DREAMS OF
A LONGING
HEART

Also by Jane Peart
in Large Print:

Homeward the Seeking Heart
The Pattern
A Perilous Bargain
The Pledge
The Promise
Shadow of Fear
Thread of Suspicion
Web of Deception

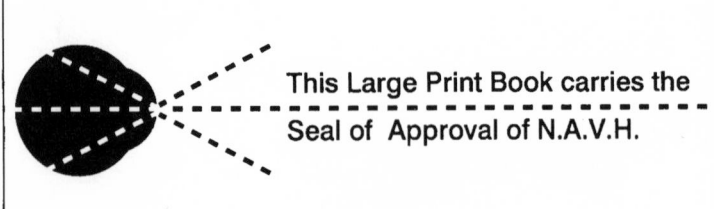

This Large Print Book carries the
Seal of Approval of N.A.V.H.

DREAMS OF
A LONGING
HEART

JANE PEART

Thorndike Press • Thorndike, Maine

Published in 2000 by arrangement with Baker Book House.

Thorndike Press Large Print Christian Fiction Series.

The tree indicium is a trademark of Thorndike Press.

The text of this Large Print edition is unabridged.
Other aspects of the book may vary from the original edition.

Set in 16 pt. Plantin.

Printed in the United States on permanent paper.

Library of Congress Cataloging-in-Publication Data

Peart, Jane.
    Dreams of a longing heart / Jane Peart.
        p. cm.
    ISBN 0-7862-2700-1 (lg. print : hc : alk. paper)
    1. Orphan trains — Fiction.   2. Women pioneers
    — Fiction.   3. Large type books. I. Title.
    PS3566.E238 D7 2000
    813'.2—dc54   00-033751

To the *real* "riders" of the orphan trains, the over 100,000 children who were transported by train across the country to new homes in the Midwest, from 1854 to the early twentieth century, whose experience and courage inspired this series.

1

Boston
Greystone Orphanage

Kit felt her toes push painfully against the end of her too-small boots. Stopping for a minute, she lifted one foot at a time and wiggled them. Grateful for the halt, her little brother leaned his small body heavily against her. The steep hill had been quite a climb for his short, five-year-old legs. Even Kit, at nearly eight, was feeling the strain and was only too happy to let Jamie rest while she herself caught her breath.

Several strides ahead of them, her father carried their baby sister, Gwynny, her round little face bobbing over his shoulder at each step.

At the top of the hill he turned around and called back to them, "Get a move on, you two. Don't be laggin' behind like that. We're almost there."

Something cold and hard lodged in Kit's chest. She was the only one of three children who knew what *there* was. Her father had explained it to her the night before.

Telling her to sit down on the other side of the kitchen table, he had leaned across it, his big workman's hands clasped tightly in front of him, and keeping his usually loud voice low, he had told her.

" 'Tis the only thing there is to do, Kit. There's no work here for me. I've got to go over to Brockton and see if I can get on at the shoe factory. And there's no one to look after you kids. They'll keep you there 'til I find a job and a place to live, then I'll come and get you."

"Why can't we come with you, Da?" Kit wanted to know.

Sean Ternan took out his red handkerchief and wiped his nose, then his eyes before answering. "There's no way I can do that, girlie. I don't even know for certain if there *is* work —" his mouth twisted as he added bitterly — "or maybe there'll be signs over there as well as here that they're not hiring *us*."

Kit knew what he meant. She had seen the postings that read: NO IRISH NEED APPLY on some of the businesses and construction sites around the city. Her father had been a journeyman bricklayer by trade in Ireland. Mam had told Kit that when he'd first come to this country as a young fellow, he'd walked

8

with a swagger, sure of himself, sure he could make a good living, and like so many of his countrymen, sure he'd find the proverbial pot of gold at the end of the American rainbow.

But it had all turned out so much differently. Her father was forced at length to go to work in one of the mills at low pay, long hours, subject to frequent layoffs. "Last hired, first fired" was the rule of thumb and most often it was the immigrant Irishmen who went when production fell off.

Things had gone from bad to worse the last two years. After Gwynny's birth Kit's mother, Eileen, had sickened and three months ago she had died. Soon after this, Sean Ternan had lost his job.

Her father's voice echoed in the empty street, jarring her back to the dark, chilly morning, the frightening present.

"Kit, come along, girl. We've not got all day!"

She tugged at her brother's hand. "Come on, Jamie, it's not far now," she encouraged.

"I'm tired, Kit. Hungry, too."

"Like as not, they'll give us something to eat when we get there," Kit assured him. Her own stomach felt hollow. She hadn't been able to eat much of the oatmeal she had fixed for them all before they left the flat earlier. There was a heavy lump in her throat that would not go away, over which she could not swallow more than a spoonful of oatmeal.

Jamie dragged on her as they trudged along, trying to catch up with their tall father.

"I'm cold," he whimpered.

Kit pressed her lips together. She wanted to scold him. *Shut up! I'm cold and tired, too. But there's worse waiting for us where we're going!* But she couldn't. Her heart was too sore, aching with the knowledge that was *her* burden, not her little brother's.

Then suddenly she saw the black iron arch over the gate. Even though Kit had to leave school to take care of the younger children when her mother died, she had kept up with her reading and now she could make out the words on the sign:

GREYSTONE COUNTY ORPHANAGE

For the first time something inside Kit rebelled. "But *we're* not orphans!" Suddenly she ran forward, the reluctant Jamie stumbling after her. When she reached her father, she looked up at him, tried to slip her cold, ungloved hand into his.

But he was staring straight ahead, his face like granite. Kit followed the direction of his glance and saw his lips moving silently. Sean

10

Ternan was also reading the sign.

A minute later they were standing on the stone steps in front of a massive door and he was ringing the bell. It was answered by a harried-looking girl in a mobcap and blue-checkered apron, and they stepped inside the front door. The next thing Kit knew they were ushered through a door marked HEAD MATRON, MISS AGATHA CLINOCK. There a severe-looking, gray-haired woman behind the desk was regarding them all over glasses that pinched her rather large nose.

Kit heard Father say, " 'Tis only temporary, you see, ma'am. As soon as I've found work, I intend to come back for my family. I promised my wife, God rest her soul, that I'd do my best to keep us all together."

Miss Clinock inclined her head slightly, fingering the black cord that hung from her glasses to a pin on the starched front of a high-necked gray blouse.

"Of course, Mr. Ternan. You understand, we are obliged to give *temporary* shelter to children of indigent families, but we make very clear it is for six months *only*. If they are not reunited with their parents by then, we are forced to seek suitable adoptive homes for them. This institution is almost at its capacity now. You were fortunate, indeed, that we are able to

11

provide for *three* children at this time."

Kit's father nodded, his hands twisting nervously. Gwynny was sucking her thumb, Jamie fidgeting. Kit felt stiff, as if she had turned to wood. She could not take her eyes off her father. He looked at her once and his eyes were shiny. Then he turned his head and would not look her way again.

Another woman in a black dress and gray apron opened the office door, summoned as if by magic, and Miss Clinock spoke to her.

"These are the Ternan children, Miss Massey. The little girl goes to Nursery, the boy to Primary and —" She scrutinized Kit. "How old are you, child?" she asked.

"Seven," Kit murmured shyly.

"Speak up, child, don't mumble," Miss Clinock corrected.

"She's near eight. Smart as a whip." Kit's father said, his voice sounding almost too loud and hearty.

"All right then, take her to Third," Miss Clinock directed.

Her father lifted Gwynny out of his lap, set her on her feet, gently shoving her toward Miss Massey who stood waiting at the open office door. When Gwynny did not budge, he spoke to Kit.

"Take her hand, Kit. She'll go with you."

Kit heard a roaring in her ears, not real-

12

izing it was her own heart pounding frantically.

"It will be all right, mind you." Her father's voice sounded as if it came from a long distance. "Jamie, lad, do as you're told. Now, Kit, go along."

Kit felt strong fingers clamp on her thin shoulder, turning her around to face the door. Gwynny's soft little hand curled into her palm. Kit took one or two hesitant steps, then looked back at her father. She halted, desperately hoping that somehow this was all a mistake, that he would gather them all up and out they'd go, away from this strange, grim place.

But Sean Ternan was sitting like a stone in the chair opposite Miss Clinock's desk, looking down at his hands. He neither moved nor spoke.

"Goodbye, Da!" Kit called over her shoulder, her voice cracking a little.

They were out in the hall now, and Miss Massey closed the office door firmly. Then, placing a clammy hand on Kit's neck, she urged her forward.

"Go along, child," she ordered and Kit looked down a long corridor of gray walls to which there seemed to be no end.

2

Meadowridge

Cora Hansen came out of church into the bright April sunshine and, calling her three younger boys from their play under the budding maple trees in the churchyard, went straight over to their wagon where the two horses were hitched to the fence. She helped the boys into the back, then she climbed up into the wooden seat in front. Shivering, she pulled her shawl around her thin rounded shoulders. Seems like she was always cold, even on a warm day like this.

She'd left her husband talking to some of the other farmers outside the church. Not that Jess was one to socialize much. Just getting him in town to church on Sundays was about all Cora could manage. But since the individual farms around Meadowridge were all pretty isolated from one another and the men busy from sunup until the last chore was done at sunset, Sunday after service was about the only time they had to congregate, discuss the weather, crops and livestock.

Usually Cora took advantage of this to pass the time of day with some of the other wives. It was her only chance to visit because Jess didn't like her going off to the quilting bees or the get-togethers for canning or jelly-making like some of the others did.

"Too much gossipin' and gabbin' and meddlin' in other folks' business," he would say. "You got enough to keep you busy at home with the young'uns and your own chores."

Whether that was true or not of those gatherings, what Jess thought became law in the Hansen household, and Cora had always gone along with whatever Jess thought.

But this Sunday she had not stopped to speak to the few women she knew because she had some thinking to do, and she needed to be by herself to sort out her thoughts.

Most of the time during the sermon, Cora's mind was on the Sunday meal she would have to get on the table the minute they got home from church. But this time there wasn't Reverend Brewster's familiar drone to lull her into a half-attentive state. Instead, an earnest young man from the Rescuers and Providers Society riveted them all with dramatic stories of city children lost and abandoned, without homes or families. He had ended with a plea that Cora simply could not put out of her mind. Especially since responding to it seemed a way of solving her own problem.

At thirty-five, Cora looked a good dozen years older. Her straight hair, the color of a field mouse, was pulled straight back into a knot. Her skin was parched-looking, etched with sun-squint wrinkles around her lackluster eyes. She was worn-out, overworked, had an acid tongue and an attitude to match.

She had married Jess, a widower twelve years older than she, when she was fifteen. That was twenty years ago. Now there were five children, all boys.

Cora rarely thought about her life in any conscious way. She had come out West as a nine-year-old child with her father, two brothers, and their stepmother. Lured by the promise of gold in the hills around Meadowridge, her pa had prospected for a few years with no luck. He had then turned to homesteading and a safer life, if no easier. It had also proved no more profitable.

As a child Cora grew up working alongside her brothers — hoeing, sowing, weeding. It had been a joyless, dirt-poor, bone-tiring childhood, but it was all she knew. When her father died her stepmother had sold the land to Jess Hansen, whose property adjoined theirs. Jess had already built a house and barn and wanted the additional acreage to provide extra grazing pasture.

Cora's stepmother, who was glad to pack up and leave the sod house, give up the endless struggle, the cold winters, to go back to her kin in Tennessee, had told Cora, "You kin come with me, or stay."

Since Cora had never gotten along with her stepmother, it did not take her long to decide to accept Jess's laconic offer of marriage. She had moved from her father's home into her husband's without much change from the relentless drudgery and monotony of life she had always known.

Until now, she had never expected anything to be different. Until today, when she heard that man from the Providers and Rescuers Society talk about taking an orphan into your home. She could sure use some help. Cora straightened her hunched shoulders, unconsciously easing the almost constant ache in her back. It bothered her just as much sitting as standing, whether she was lugging in buckets of water from the well or full milk pails from the barn. Years of back-breaking work had begun to take their toll.

Even the two big boys were not much help

with her chores. Jess had them working alongside him in the fields now. And the three little ones couldn't do a whole lot except feed the chickens, gather eggs, and do some occasional weeding.

What she needed was a good, strong girl to take some of the load — somebody to churn, help with the canning, haul out the heavy baskets of laundry on washday.

But what would Jess say to them taking in one of them orphans? From what the speaker said, the Society would provide enough clothing for them for a year until the family who took them decided whether or not to adopt them. All the family had to do was feed them, bed them, see that they got their schooling and attended Sunday service.

They certainly had enough room, Cora knew. The attic had plenty of space to put a cot up there, and another mouth to feed on a farm was no problem. In fact, with some help, Cora figured she could put in a bigger vegetable garden.

Just then Cora saw Jess heading for the wagon. He had rounded up the two older boys who had been playing with some of their friends from Sunday school. Cora decided to wait until after they had eaten their big Sunday midday meal before broaching the subject of taking in one of the orphans when the train came through Meadowridge. He'd be in a better mood then, more likely to see things her way.

3

Orphan Train
En Route to the Midwest

"No one will ever adopt me," Kit said to herself, staring out the window as the train roared through the flat Kansas prairie. No matter what Mrs. Scott said, Kit was sure of it. She was too tall, too skinny, too shy. Hadn't they made three stops already, all the children lined up on the station platform, while groups of people in each of the towns walked around, looking at them, making comments to each other — sometimes behind hands held over their mouths, other times right out loud?

Kit had tried to smile, although she was careful not to show her teeth, because she had a space between her two front ones. Some of the boys teased her, calling her "snaggletooth." And she had made her eyes wide to look alert and intelligent.

Still, so far, she was among the ones marched back on the train to settle in for another long ride until the next town. Each time, the certainty that no one would ever want her lodged more stubbornly in her heart.

Kit looked over to where Toddy was organizing some of the children for a game. Maybe if she were lively and clever like Toddy, or pretty like Laurel — Kit sighed. She remembered that day at Greystone, the first time she realized what "adoption" meant.

It was during recess and they were all out in the fenced-in side playground. Kit was taking turns skipping rope when someone had yelled, "Come look!" They had all rushed over to the fence in time to see a carriage pull up in front of the main entrance and watched as a well-dressed couple got out and climbed the steps into the building.

"Who do you think they are?" Toddy had wondered aloud.

"Somebody's parents coming to get them?" suggested Laurel, an edge of longing in her voice.

"No, stupid!" Molly B. retorted disdainfully, her freckled face pressed like the others against the wire fence, gawking at the strangers. "They're folks come to visit the Nursery and pick out a baby."

"What do you mean?" Kit asked through stiff lips.

"Just what I said, ninny." Molly B. turned to Kit, squinting her eyes and making a face. "They're gonna take one home with them, what did ya think I meant? They always pick the little ones, ya know. The cutest ones."

Kit felt her stomach lurch sickly. Immediately, she thought of Gwynny, with her rosy cheeks and dimpled smile and tumbled curls. Surely they wouldn't let Gwynny be adopted! Not when their Da was coming back for them all soon!

Her terror must have shown on her face because Molly B., smelling the scent of fear, lunged for an attack.

"Bet your little sister'll be 'dopted," she smirked.

Kit left the fence. She heard Toddy defy Molly B. "What do *you* know?" And the next thing Kit felt was Toddy and Laurel on either side of her, walking her away from the sound of Molly B.'s taunting voice.

"I been here longer than any of you, and I do so know! The Nursery babies *always* get 'dopted!"

That was on a Thursday. On Sundays at Greystone, children with brothers or sisters in the other sections were allowed a "family visit." As long as she had been at Greystone, Kit had looked forward to Sundays when she could see Jamie and little Gwynny.

It had surprised her to see how quickly Jamie had settled in at Greystone and that he actually seemed happy. But, of course, he was with other boys for the first time in his life. When their mother was ill and after she died, Jamie had been confined to their small tenement flat with only his baby sister and Kit. Kit, placed in charge of the two younger ones while their father was at work, burdened as she was with grown-up responsibility, tended to be "bossy," Jamie complained. He had chafed under her care. Now he was experiencing a kind of freedom, a well-ordered life, three meals a day, boisterous play with companions his own age and sex.

Jamie became restless and bored during their family visits. Even Gwynny squirmed down from Kit's lap after a few minutes and seemed just as willing to go back to the Nursery when the hour was up. This hurt Kit's feelings more than she cared to admit. She prayed their Da would come soon so that they could be a family again. But with each passing week that hope grew dimmer, and Kit felt a strange uneasiness.

The Sunday following the day she had seen that couple arrive, Kit went as usual to meet her brother and sister. Only Jamie was waiting for her.

"Where's Gwynny?" she asked, the words

almost choking her.

Jamie shrugged and said, "Dunno. When I stopped at the Nursery to bring her over, Miss Driscoll told me she was on a 'probation visit.' "

"A probation visit? What's that?" Kit gasped.

Jamie shrugged again. "Dunno. That's all she told me."

Kit grabbed him by the shoulders and shook him. "What's the matter with you, Jamie? Why didn't you ask? Find out? That's our Gwynny they're talking about! Where's she visiting?"

"Leggo of me, Kit! You're hurting me!" Jamie shouted, wriggling out of her grip.

Kit dropped her hands, clenching them into fists. "I'm sorry, Jamie. I didn't mean to hurt you. But listen to me!" Hot tears were stinging her eyes now. "We got to find out about Gwynny, don't you see that? What if Da comes and finds her gone?"

Jamie rubbed his shoulder and glared at her. "Da's not coming back," he mumbled.

"That's a wicked thing to say, Jamie."

"It's true." Jamie protested. "We're all goin' to get 'dopted."

"It's *not* true and Da *is* goin' to come back. He promised!" Kit said more to herself than to her brother. "Who told you such a thing?"

"My friend Tom. He heard 'em talkin', them people that come to look at the babies the other day. He's been here since he was two and he told me that we're way past 'temporary' now. That means you either stay here or else you get 'dopted. Boys are more likely to get 'dopted than girls."

Kit swallowed. Her mouth felt dry with fear. Somehow what Jamie was saying rang true. She'd heard much the same kind of talk among the girls in her section. It had been months since their father had brought them here. She had tried to keep track of the time, but somehow she had gotten mixed up. That cold, sick churning began in her stomach again.

"Can I go now?" Jamie asked. "We wuz goin' to play ball 'fore I had to come over here —" He slid off the bench and hopped from one foot to the other.

Kit nodded. There was no reason for him to stay any longer. Sadly she watched him push through the gate and start running. Suddenly Kit was clutched with an awful fear that she might never see him again, and she jumped up. Flinging herself against the fence, she called his name. But Jamie kept on running and didn't look back.

"He must not have heard me," Kit said to herself.

Remembering that scene, Kit felt her throat constrict. Two weeks later Jamie, too, was adopted. When she was told, Kit burst into tears.

"What will my Da say when he comes and they're not here?" she had asked, almost hysterical.

Finally Miss Clinock told her as gently as possible that her father had been notified of both Gwynny's and Jamie's adoption requests and had signed their releases.

"Then, is he comin' for *me?*" was her next question.

"I'm sorry, Kit, but I'm afraid not," the matron said quietly.

And now Kit had a chance to be adopted, too. Mrs. Scott had assured her they had only chosen the most suitable children to take on the Orphan Train, ones that would fit in nicely with the families that had agreed to adopt. But Kit's uncertainty lingered. If her own Da had not wanted her, who would?

4

Meadowridge

Cora Hansen lifted the heavy blue enameled coffeepot from the stove, brought it to the table, and refilled her husband's cup. Jess was scraping the last of the sausage and eggs onto his fork, helping it along with the remainder of a biscuit held in his other hand.

Setting it back down on the stove, Cora took a seat across from him. Crossing her arms on top of the table, she leaned forward.

"You'll be sure to quit afore noon so's we can eat and get into town in time, won't you?" she asked anxiously. She was worried, had been all along, that Jess might change his mind about them taking in a girl from the Orphan Train.

He didn't answer, just continued to chew, not looking up from his plate.

"Jess? You didn't forget, did you? Today's the day that Orphan Train gets here. We need to get into town early so's we can look 'em all over good."

Jess wiped his mouth with the back of his

hand, then pushed his chair away from the table. He looked at his wife with narrowed eyes.

"You shure you want to go through with this? Don't seem like we need no other child 'round here."

"I told you, Jess. It'll be like havin' another pair of hands. There's enough work for two women here now with five young'uns, the garden, and all. And especially come harvest time, when we have the hired workers to feed. I mean to pick out a half-growed girl, strong, sturdy. She'll be a big help. You'll see."

In spite of everything, her anxiety that after all the talking she'd done to persuade him might not be enough, trembled in her voice.

"I'll lose pretty near a day's work goin' into town in the middle of the week like this," he grumbled.

"It'll be just this once, Jess."

"We gotta sign some papers, don't we? Put money out?"

"No, Jess, I explained it to you. We've jest got to agree that she gets her schoolin', gets fed and dressed proper. And we make two reports a year to the Society that she's bein' taken care of — until she's eighteen. That's all there is to it."

28

Jess stood up and walked toward the back door. With his hand on the knob, he turned and fixed a level gaze on his wife for a long minute.

"Well, if you're sure we ain't takin' on mor'n we can handle — It's up to you. I got my hands full with the farm and the live-stock. The boys ain't that much good in the fields yet —"

"Oh, she'll pull her weight. I'll see to that," Cora assured him as she followed him out onto the back porch, wiping her hands on her blue checkered apron. "She'll do her share of the chores. You don't have to fret none about that."

Jess grunted again, clomped down the steps and started toward the barn.

Cora sighed with relief. Satisfied that there'd be no last-minute hitch, she went back inside. She hurried over to clear the table of her husband's plate and cup. Then she set out bowls and went over to the stove to stir the pot of oatmeal.

As she stirred Cora stared out the kitchen window. It was getting light now. The chil-dren would be waking up soon, coming down to eat. One thing that girl could do when she came was cook the kids' breakfast.

Cora sighed again. She couldn't imagine what it would be like to have some of the burden lifted from her — the constant round of chores, going from one thing to the other with never a breathing space between.

Of course, come fall, the girl would have to go into school every day with Lonny and Caspar and little Seth. They'd had to agree to that in order to get one of the orphans. But it was in summer that farm work was heaviest anyway, and then Cora's chores would be lightened considerably with someone young and strong to help.

Cora wondered what it would be like to have another female around. She was used to a houseful of boys and no other woman for miles around to talk to. Not that she meant to make a fuss over the girl. That wouldn't do. They were giving a homeless girl a permanent roof over her head, and that was more than she had now.

Cora had always felt herself an "outsider" among the Meadowridge folks somehow. As if she weren't as good as some of the women who lived in town. It gave her a smug feeling that the Hansens were among the families willing to offer to shelter "these poor abandoned waifs" Mr. Scott had talked about.

Not that she had gone to a lot of trouble getting ready for the orphan. But she *had* fixed up a place for the girl. Cleared out the clutter from a corner of the attic to make a sleeping room. She'd been careful not to ask Jess for anything extra. Just got out the old iron bedstead that had been stored there since goodness knows when, cleaned it, and made it up with muslin sheets and some of her older quilts. It wasn't much, but probably better than the girl was used to in whatever orphanage she come from. Surely she wouldn't expect too much.

Besides, she'd learn soon enough that the Hansens were plain folks, living a simple farm family's life. They were offering the girl a sight better than her own childhood had been, Cora thought, remembering the sod house she'd lived in with her family before she'd married Jess and moved into the frame house.

They'd added on rooms as the children had come along, and it was as nice as most of the other farmhouses around. Well, maybe not so fancy as some who had put in parlors and front porches. Of course, no use for them to have either one. Jess didn't hold with having company, so buying that mail-order parlor furniture would have been a waste of money. He put most of what they earned from their crops right back into buying good livestock and better farm implements. And he wanted to build a new barn —

Cora's thoughts were interrupted by the sound of bare feet running down wooden steps as the two older boys came tumbling into the kitchen, tussling with each other as they usually did.

"Now, you boys, stop that carryin' on and set down and eat," she ordered.

The two rumpled-haired boys, ages nine and ten, stopped jostling each other, pulled up their overall straps and slid into their seats, thumping their elbows onto the table.

"Where are the others?" Cora demanded as she spooned cereal into their bowls.

"Seth's comin'. Chet and Tom's still sleepin'." Caspar replied, grabbing a spoon.

"Well, they'll have to git up. We all got to go into town today and fetch that girl who's comin' to live here."

Both boys looked up in surprise. "You mean that girl from the *Orphan Train* you been talkin' about gettin'?" Lonny stopped eating long enough to ask.

"The very one," Cora answered briskly. "Now eat up. You got to feed the chickens and collect the eggs afore we go."

"How long is she goin' to stay, Ma?"

"She's goin' to *live* here, for pity's sake."

"Forever?" Caspar persisted.

"Well, I should think so. At least 'til she's full-growed. I'm sure she won't want to go back to that orphan asylum. I expect she'd have to be pretty miserable to want to do *that!*" Cora said sarcastically, adding, "I should think she'll like livin' on a farm after where she's been."

Turning back to the stove, Cora missed the sly look the boys exchanged. A look of silent consent, mischievous intent, a look of mixed anticipation and malice, a look that implied trouble for their unsuspecting victim — the girl from the Orphan Train.

5

Summer, 1890

"Come along, Kit, you've been adopted!"

Kit turned around and looked up at Mrs. Scott; her heart gave an excited little jump.

"I have?" she exclaimed, slipping down from the chair she'd been sitting on so long, tense with anxiety as one after the other of her fellow orphans had been selected and taken out of the Social Hall to their new homes. Her secret fear that she was too plain, too tall, too skinny for anyone to want was laid to rest. She had seen Toddy happily skip away with the elegantly dressed woman and the pretty, dark-eyed older girl. Then Laurel had left, hand in hand, with the doctor who had examined them all. Kit had been the only one of the trio remaining.

"Yes, you are going with the Hansen family. They live on a farm just outside Meadowridge. But you'll be coming into town to go to school, so you'll be seeing Toddy and Laurel again soon." Mrs. Scott seemed a little nervous as she helped Kit gather up her things.

Kit had read stories about farms. They had always sounded so nice. Now she was going to live on one!

Mrs. Scott took Kit's hand and led her over to where a tall man stood with Reverend Brewster and Mr. Scott on the other side of the room. As they approached, the man turned and stared at Kit. Kit's fingers gripped Mrs. Scott's hand tightly as she met the man's narrowed gaze.

But Jess Hansen didn't look like any of the farmers Kit had read about. Those storybook characters had been jolly and kind, working hard, but coming in at noon and night to eat hearty meals with the family. This Mr. Hansen looked as if he had eaten a sour pickle! He had a sallow face and thin lips that curled when he spoke. Lank, wheat-colored hair fell in a shock over his forehead, and he brushed it back impatiently from his dull, deep-set eyes.

"This is Kathleen Ternan, Mr. Hansen," Mrs. Scott introduced Kit, loosening Kit's clinging grasp and pushing her gently toward him.

Jess gave a brief nod, then stuffing the papers he had just signed into his coat pocket, he jerked his head toward the door and said gruffly, "Well, then, let's git goin'."

"She's called Kit, Mr. Hansen. I'm sure you'll find her sweet-natured, obedient and willing," Mrs. Scott began, but Jess was already moving toward the door.

Mrs. Scott bent down and took Kit's face in both hands and kissed her cheek. "You'll be fine, Kit, don't worry. Any family would be lucky to get you. I'm sure Mrs. Hansen will love having a little girl since she has five boys. So you'll be a welcome addition."

Kit's heart was hammering now. She wasn't at all sure she wanted to go with this unpleasant man, even if he *did* live on a farm.

"Come on," Jess called from the doorway.

Mrs. Scott gave her a final hug. "Go ahead, Kit, and God bless you!"

Kit hurried toward the tall man waiting for her. At the door she turned for one last look at Mrs. Scott and tried to smile. Mrs. Scott waved encouragingly and Kit waved back, then followed Jess outside.

It was hard for Kit, lugging her suitcase, to keep up with his long strides as Jess headed for a buckboard hitched to the rail fence. He untied his horse and climbed up into the wagon seat.

"Well, come on, girl, git in!" he called to Kit, standing a few feet away. *Cora's going to be mad as a wet hen when she sees the size of her,* Jess thought grumpily.

Things hadn't gone right all day. It was bad enough that he'd got a late start coming into town. Not that it was his fault. One of the boys had left the pasture gate open and three of the cows had got out. It had taken him the good part of an hour to round them up again. Jess felt the anger rise in him again. Neither one had owned up to doing it, so he'd had to lick both of them.

All that had taken so much time, he'd sat down late to the midday dinner. And had no peace then with Cora, persimmon-lipped, banging pots and pans around to show she was upset with the delay. It was a miserable meal and he'd had indigestion 'fore he finished.

Cora was so distracted with her fuming that she hadn't been paying attention to what she was doing, and the smallest young'un got too near the stove and pulled a pot of soaking beans over on himself.

At that point Cora had told Jess to go on without her. She had to see to the mess on the floor, and the child had to be tended to. So Cora, busy with scolding the boy and cleaning everything up, couldn't go along with him.

The last thing Jess had heard as he pulled

out in the wagon had been Cora's strident voice yelling from the kitchen window, "Now you can see why I need help, can't you?"

Well, Cora was going to be none too happy with the girl he was bringing home, Jess thought morosely. She wanted a strong, strapping girl and this one — Jess shook his head — why she looked like a strong wind might blow her down.

But when he'd finally got to where they had all them orphans, there were just a few of them left. No boys at all. Jess would have preferred a boy himself, one twelve, fourteen, big enough to really give him a hand with the farm chores. But Cora had been pickin' and naggin' and complainin' so that he'd been wore out with hearin' it and there weren't nuthin' to do but give in.

"You deaf, girl?" He'd frowned down at Kit. "I said, git in!" His tone was irritable.

Struggling with her cardboard suitcase, the coat she hadn't had a chance to put on slung over her arm, Kit grabbed the handle on the side of the wagon with her free hand and hoisted herself up beside Jess. Her bonnet had slid off and was dangling by its ribbons around her neck. But before she could secure it or was hardly settled on the narrow plank seat, Jess flicked the reins and the wagon jerked forward. Kit had to grip tight to the rough sides to keep her balance as they rumbled through the streets of Meadowridge and headed out of town.

She hadn't even been able to say a proper goodbye to either Toddy or Laurel, Kit thought sadly. But Mrs. Scott had assured her that they would see each other often, that they would be going to the same school and church.

"We will keep track of all of you to see how you're doing, you know!" she had told Kit comfortingly.

As they left the town behind, Kit became aware of her surroundings. The road had narrowed and everywhere she looked were fields and meadows and orchards, stretching as far as she could see on either side.

Kit had grown up in a grimy, industrial city, its air thick with acrid odors spewed out in yellow-gray clouds from factory smokestacks, darkening the atmosphere, obscuring the sunshine. Before Greystone, all she had known was the small, crowded tenement flat, its labyrinthine halls and dark stairways heavy with the greasy smells of cooking cabbage, the musty smell of rotting wood, airless passages.

What she was seeing was all new to her

and she breathed deeply of the pure, clean country air, scented delicately with the blossoming apple trees in the orchards beside the road.

It was all so beautiful! Kit felt delight swell inside her, a pleasure she had never experienced before spread all through her body. She could not resist smiling, enjoying each new thing she noticed, the grazing cows who looked up as the wagon rolled by, a hillside of fluffy sheep with a few lambs trotting alongside the big ones, a pasture where several horses ran tossing their manes.

Kit started to point and exclaim at everything she saw, then glanced over at the silent man beside her. He was staring straight ahead, his face like one of those wooden Indians Kit had once seen in front of a store. So Kit swallowed her excitement and they rode on with never a word spoken the whole way.

Cora had been to the kitchen window at least a dozen times. Shielding her eyes from the afternoon sun with her hand, she searched down the lane to the road for some sign of the returning wagon. Where in the world was Jess?

Gradually Cora's uneasiness turned to

anger. If he had got into town too late and missed being in time to get one of them orphan girls — her thought drifted away unfinished as just then she saw, rounding the turn of the road in the distance, the familiar wagon rolling into sight.

She watched as it rattled up toward the house and strained to get a good look at the figure sitting beside Jess on the open wagon seat. As it came closer Cora's hands balled into fists. Standing on the edge of the porch, she stiffened as Jess reined the horse to a stop. Without looking at his wife, he got down and came around the other side of the wagon. There he stood, hands hanging at his side, while a little girl climbed gingerly down.

My land! Cora bit her lip. Disappointment and frustration battled with rising fury. What was Jess thinking of? Bringing home a wisp of a girl like that? Why, she didn't look hardly stronger than Seth. Not fit to do a day's worth of chores, if Cora was any judge.

She threw Jess a withering look as the two of them approached the porch. At the bottom of the steps they both halted.

"This here's Kit," mumbled Jess, jerking his thumb at the child.

Cora heard the rush of the boys running

out from the house behind her to stand staring curiously at their father and the little girl.

Cora wrestled helplessly for words. She wanted to dress down her husband proper for his lack of good sense. She might as well have no one as this slip of a thing. It would be just another mouth to feed, a child to cope with! He must have been plumb out of his mind to take this one.

While she struggled Cora wondered if they could return her, or had the Orphan Train already left, after depositing its passengers?

"Is that her?" Caspar demanded in a loud voice.

"Is that our orphan?" asked Lonny.

Cora felt the younger boys clinging to her apron. The stunned silence lengthened agonizingly.

Then for the first time Cora let herself look directly at the girl. She was startled to see wide, clear eyes — the color of a mourning dove's wing — regarding her. Then the child smiled a spontaneous, radiant smile that transformed her small, plain face. Momentarily unsettled by its warmth, Cora spoke brusquely.

"Well, you might as well come in. Supper's near ready."

She'd deal with Jess later, she decided. See what could be done about this terrible mistake.

"I'll show you where to put your things," she said, bustling into the house. Still lugging her belongings, Kit followed more slowly. Motioning Kit by the line of gawking boys, Cora led the way up the stairway to the second floor. There she stopped and, opening a wooden door, stepped aside and indicated a narrower flight of steps to the attic.

"Up there's your place," she told Kit. "When you've washed up, you can come down and eat."

Breathless by now from the climb, Kit went the rest of the way up alone. When she reached the top, she dropped her suitcase, flexed her cramped fingers, and looked around.

Under the slanted ceiling was a small, black iron bed with a white coverlet and a striped blanket folded at the end. There was a pine chest with a tiny mirror above it. On top was a plain white pottery washbowl and pitcher, and a dish with a cake of yellow soap. On the wall hung a wooden rack with a washcloth and two towels. A small bench was placed under the window, set into the eaves.

Kit walked over to the window and, unlatching it, pushed it open. Leaning her elbows on the sill, she looked out.

She had never seen anything like it! The sun was just touching the treetops around the farmhouse with a golden haze, and beyond it squares of farmland, all different shades of green, spread out before her like a patchwork quilt. The air, sweet and dewy fresh, rose into her nostrils, and Kit inhaled it as though it were some kind of rare exotic perfume.

A new emotion suffused Kit's very being. If it was not quite happiness, erasing all the old sadnesses, the constant aching wonder about Jamie and Gwynny, it did fill Kit with a nameless joy. It was a sense of discovery, of finding something she had not even known existed.

Taking another long breath, Kit turned from the window and glanced around with satisfaction. She had never before had a room to herself, a room all her own! Kit sighed with contentment. Oh, how lucky she was to be "placed out" here!

6

Kit shook out a clean sheet from the pile in the basket and, stretching up her arms, pinned it awkwardly to the line.

All morning she had helped Cora with the washing. They had begun right after breakfast. First, carrying bucket after bucket of water from the well into the house and pouring it into big pots to heat on the stove. Then Cora had posted her at the kitchen stove to watch until the water began to boil. When that happened, she was to lift it carefully and take it out to the side of the house, where Cora was bent over a huge, copper tub set on a wooden sawhorse, scrubbing vigorously on a metal washboard. It was hot, heavy work on this warm summer day.

When each load was done, it was piled into a big oak-chip basket and Kit was told to hang the wet laundry on the hemp rope, strung in lines from the corner of the house to posts near the fence. Kit liked being outside in the sunshine better than inside. Out here, the fresh breeze brought the sweet smells of wildflowers and turned earth from the fields beyond.

As she worked Kit thought about her life with the Hansens.

Jess had hardly said a word to her since she had arrived, barely acknowledged her presence. Even at mealtimes when she sat down after placing the serving bowls on the table, he never so much as glanced her way.

Mealtimes were silent affairs. That seemed strange to Kit and not at all the way she had thought it would be in a family. Her own family had been different. Even though they had been poor and the meals never as abundant as here at the Hansens, there had been lots of talk. Before her Mam had taken sick, she and Da carried on long conversations. Kit didn't remember what they had been about, but she remembered laughter and a warmth that was lacking here.

There never seemed to be any laughter at the Hansens. Unless you'd call laughter the boisterous jeering of Caspar and Lonny when they'd played some kind of trick on her.

Tricks and teasing were a way of life here at the Hansens, Kit was beginning to accept. Those two were always doing something to make things difficult for her — whether it was slyly kicking over the basket of beans she'd been sent to pick out in the vegetable garden, or sneaking up to her room and putting a frog inside her shoe so that she'd let out a shriek when she slipped her foot into it first thing in the morning. Worse still, was the time they had put a dead mouse in her pitcher and it had plunked into her washbowl when she poured in the water.

She never knew when the next attack was coming. Even though she was growing more wary, she hadn't always been able to second-guess the devilment the two boys between them could devise.

But she never tattled on them. Kit had learned at Greystone never to "snitch" on anyone. But instead of discouraging the boys, that only seemed to egg them on to worse mischief. Where no punishment was inflicted, the persecution continued.

Why didn't they like her? Kit wondered, sighing as she dragged another heavy damp sheet out of the big wicker basket and struggled to hang it straight. She had made some headway with the *little* boys, even Seth, the middle one, who wanted to tag along with his big brothers, only they wouldn't let him. But the rest of the Hansens, including Cora, seemed cold and distant.

It certainly wasn't how Mrs. Scott had said "placing out" would be like. With the familiar twinge in her heart, Kit thought

47

about Jamie and Gwynny. She wondered where they were and how they were getting along in their new homes. She missed them awfully. She hoped they were loved and well cared for. She knew Jamie would love being on a farm like this with all the animals — the baby chicks and the ducklings down at the pond, the new calves. If she knew where he was, she could write and tell him about them. None of the Hansens seemed to think any of this was special at all.

Kit felt dreadfully lonely sometimes, with no one to talk to. She particularly missed her Greystone friends, Laurel and Toddy. She saw them once a week at Sunday school when she went into town to church with the Hansens. But they did not have much time then to be together to talk.

Kit sighed. She could tell that Toddy and Laurel were happy in *their* new homes. Laurel wore such pretty dresses, and Toddy was always talking about the big house on the hill where she lived now as Helene Hale's "little sister."

Kit thought back to the day of the Fourth of July. She had been surprised to learn that the Hansens were going into the town park for the annual picnic. There was a flurry of extra baking that morning. Pies and a cake were set out to cool and a ham brought out of the cellar. Cora was up at dawn getting things ready, packing the big wicker hamper with their food. While Cora stewed, Jess grumbled more than usual, and Lonny and Caspar ran in and out of the house to the wagon that had been hitched up early and brought around to the back.

The three smaller boys were underfoot in the kitchen, getting in the way, impatiently asking, "When are we goin' to go?" until their mother snapped, "When *I'm* good and ready! Quit that whinin' and go git in the wagon, or you won't go at all!"

Kit stood quietly, awaiting directions, as Cora's eyes swung around the kitchen, checking to see if anything could possibly have been forgotten. Kit had learned not to ask too many questions. Her new mother did not like to be anticipated nor did she like suggestions.

Finally she said, "Well, I 'spose that's it. Iffen we forgot sumpin', it'll have to be forgot."

With this, she picked up her sunbonnet and tied it firmly under her chin, took down her shawl from its peg on the door, then motioned Kit to take the other handle of the hamper. Together, they carried it out to the wagon.

All the way into town Kit looked forward

to seeing Toddy and Laurel, who told her they would both be there. Caspar and Lonny had whispered behind their hands, giggling mischievously, and Kit felt sure they were plotting something. But the day itself had been fun. Especially when she had had dessert with the Woodwards at their picnic spot. Laurel's new "mother" was so pretty, with a sweet face and kind eyes. But when she had come over to ask Cora if Kit could go with them to watch the fireworks from the Hales' veranda, Cora had said no. She had been very abrupt, as if she didn't like Mrs. Woodward at all. It had been a real disappointment to Kit to have to leave with the Hansens. But Mrs. Woodward had leaned down and kissed her and whispered, "There'll be another time, Kit, I promise." So maybe there would be. Anyway, she could hope.

At last the overflowing laundry basket was empty, and Kit picked it up and started back to the house. She had just reached the porch steps when she heard a peal of hooting laughter. Whirling around, she saw the clothesline had been untied and all the clean sheets she had just finished hanging up were dragging on the dusty ground. At the same time she saw two overalled figures running down toward the barn.

Hot, helpless rage shot through Kit. She ran after the fast-disappearing boys, shouting furiously. "Just you wait!" But they were already far beyond her reach. Breathing hard, she stopped on the path, angry tears crowding into her eyes.

What could she do? Didn't they realize their own mother had spent hours doing the work they had ruined in less than a minute? Shoulders sagging, Kit turned slowly around just as Cora came out onto the porch. Seeing the drooping clothesline, the sheets in the dust, her face reddened angrily.

"Land sakes, girl, can't you even hang up clothes proper?" she demanded. "Didn't they teach you nuthin' in that orphanage?"

7

Cora wiped the beads of perspiration from her forehead with the back of one arm while she stirred the bubbling contents of the kettle — blackberries. These berries were the last of the season. The smaller boys had brought her in two full buckets of them yesterday. You couldn't let things like that go to waste. 'Specially when it was free. Blackberry jam would come in handy on buckwheat cakes, biscuits, and such come wintertime.

In this first week of September, the days were cooler, but even so the heat was getting to her. Maybe she should have had Kit do the stirring for a while instead of sending her out to weed and pick the last of the summer squash.

She turned and looked out the kitchen window and saw Kit bending over the vegetable garden, her skirt puffed out behind her like small sails in the brisk wind. Must be a sight cooler out there than in here, Cora sighed.

Cora turned back to the stove, lifted a spoonful of the dark purple liquid, examined it, then let it drip back into the pot. Still not thick enough. As she went on stirring, Cora's eyes wandered back out to Kit. She was a good girl. Minded. Didn't sass. Did her chores and whatever else Cora told her without a fuss.

She hadn't even been sullen about missing that Fourth of July thing. Cora felt real bad about that now. She could have let her go with her friends.

"If the doctor's wife just hadn't got my dander up like she did, I might have let her go," Cora argued with herself. But then maybe she'd done right by the girl after all. Going up to that big hilltop house of the Hales' might have given her ideas. They and the Woodwards — although Doc Woodward was as nice and plain-talking as could be — lived in a different world from the Hansens. And there was no use trying to mix the two.

It was sure different having a girl around. Restful. Boys were always making some kind of racket. Pushing, shoving, wrassling each other. Like to drive a person crazy with the noise sometimes.

When just the two of them were working together in the kitchen, Kit was just as quiet as could be. But she was right there when you needed her. Didn't have to be told twice. Caught on real quick to how Cora liked things done, she did.

She certainly wasn't what Cora had expected when she'd talked Jess into taking one of them Orphan Train kids. There was something unusual about Kit. Cora shook her head wondering how long Kit had been in that orphanage? And before that? *Someone* must have taught her some of the nice little ways she had. Things like fixin' up her room like she did.

Kit didn't talk much. Not about her life before the Orphan Train anyhow. And Cora didn't ask. Except that one time when she saw the picture Kit had thumbtacked over her bed. It was a picture of an angel hovering over a little boy and girl as they crossed a bridge.

Cora had gone to the attic to put away some heavy winter clothes and wool blankets in the cedar box up there. When she saw the picture, she had asked Kit about it.

"Where did you get that?"

"It was a prize at Sunday school," Kit answered shyly.

Imagine that! The girl had won a prize! And not a word to anyone about it. If one of their boys had won something, *anything*, particularly in *Sunday school*, they'd never have heard the last of it.

"Teacher give it to you?" Cora asked.

"No ma'am, I picked it out. There were three to choose from."

"You liked that one best, huh?"

"Well —" Kit seemed to hesitate, then said slowly, "It reminded me of my little brother and sister."

Unexpectedly Cora's throat tightened. She'd turned away and gone back downstairs fast. The attic had been warm on that early summer day, but not *that* hot. Not hot enough to make Cora feel suddenly suffocated, so's she couldn't get her breath.

She had walked out on the porch and stood there for a long time. Thinking. Thinking about Kit and way back to her own childhood. She stood there for another few minutes. Then she had gone into hers and Jess's bedroom downstairs, lifted the lid of the old trunk set at the foot of the bed. She knelt down, reached into it and brought out the afghan she had crocheted. It had colorful zigzag stripes. The pattern was called "Joseph's Coat." Cora had seen one like it at a County Fair and copied it. It had taken her all one winter, collecting the right colors of yarn, working on it catch-as-catch-can between her chores. But when it was finished, she had put it away and never used it. She didn't know why. It's just that Jess preferred the quilts piled on top of the bed, and

Cora had never had any woman friend to come admire it. Oh, for land's sakes, she didn't really know *why* she had not put it out for a bedspread herself!

Cora looked at it for another minute or two, then before she could change her mind, she had marched back up to the attic and handed the afghan to Kit. "Here, you might like this to put over your bed."

Kit's eyes had lighted up like twin stars.

"Oh, thank you! Thank you! It's beautiful!" she had said, running her hand over it, laying her cheek against its softness.

Recalling the incident as she stirred, Cora said out loud to herself, "Never saw a youngster so grateful for the least little thing."

Cora glanced out the window again. Kit, with a full basket of vegetables beside her, was now picking some wildflowers growing along the fence.

That evening when Kit set the table for supper, she arranged the flowers she'd picked — daisies, purple wild asters and Queen Anne's lace — in a wide-necked green bottle and placed it in the center of the table. She had found the old glass bottle half-buried in the sand near the barn and, liking the iridescent glow of it, she had washed and polished it to use as a vase.

Cora noticed, but busy pouring the jam into her jars, didn't say anything. It was nearly time to start supper. It wasn't until the boys were rounded up, Jess seated, and she and Kit began to serve that the ruckus started.

Jess had rattled off his usual mumbled blessing before meals, and the words were hardly out of his mouth before he growled, "Who put them weeds in here?"

Cora, turning around from the stove, saw Kit's face go scarlet. Caspar and Lonny clapped their hands over their mouths, pointing at Kit.

"Weeds! Lookit the weeds!" hollered Lonny.

"Betcha she thinks they're *beautiful*, jest like she does the cows!" hooted Caspar.

Cora felt a rush of rage course through her at her own children. She saw the flowers for the first time and something quickened inside her at the delicacy of their shapes, the blend of colors, the way the light struck the mottled green of the bottle.

Then it struck her forcefully that she would never have noticed if it hadn't been for Kit.

Frying pan in hand, Cora silenced the boys with a threatening look they both recognized and feared. "I think they look right

57

pretty," she said sharply. "And you boys just keep your opinion to yourself."

After supper, as she and Kit were clearing away the dishes, Cora said to her, "School will be starting soon. I've got a piece of flowered calico put back that would make up for a dress for you. Think I've got a pattern we can cut down that'll do too."

Kit murmured, "Thank you."

Nothing else was said. Nothing else needed to be said.

Cora was bewildered by her own feelings. In spite of herself, she was drawn to the girl in a way she could not understand.

Something in Cora had been frozen through the years. Now vague longings she had never expressed began to emerge. Like the hard earth in spring after a cold winter, she began to thaw.

8

Miss Millicent Cady looked over her classroom full of students in Meadowridge Grammar School. The windows were open to a gentle May breeze. Outside, beyond the schoolyard fence, she could see the faint pink of budding apple trees in the nearby orchard. The young teacher straightened her shoulders, resisting the urge to yawn. *Spring fever!* she chided herself sternly.

The children were finding it hard to concentrate, too. Every few minutes one little head or the other would glance up from the workbooks, and gaze yearningly outside.

Milly suppressed a smile. Maybe she should ring the dismissal bell early, let them go out and enjoy the beautiful afternoon. What harm would it do if she deviated from the curriculum for one day?

The County Superintendent of Schools had already made his annual visit and declared her students' progress well within the county average. Indeed, he had commended her, saying it was somewhat above average in some cases. He had complimented her on her students' grasp of the subjects on which he had quizzed them and their remarkable performance during the Spelling Bee.

It had been a good year, all told, Milly had to admit. Maybe the best of her six years of teaching in Meadowridge. Last year she had felt restless, had wondered if it might not be a good idea to make a change, apply to another district for a new position. She realized teachers got stale. She was still under thirty, and not married. Perhaps it was time for her to move on while she was young enough to seek new horizons.

But she had stayed on and now she was glad she had. If she had not, she would not have experienced the restored enthusiasm for teaching, the unexpected joy in her profession, brought about by the entrance into her classroom of three interesting new pupils.

Milly's eyes rested on Laurel, Toddy and Kit — the Orphan Train trio — as she called them privately.

She recalled her own reservations when she had first heard they were coming. Milly had heard stories of the dire conditions from which some of the orphans came and had been apprehensive of their influence on the rest of the children.

After all, who knew what their background might be? What bad habits they had picked up. What ingrained attitudes might they bring with them? How would they fit in with the Meadowridge children? But none of her anxious premonitions were confirmed. Instead, the three little girls had proved themselves valuable additions to the class.

In spite of priding herself on never having any favorites among her students, no "teacher's pet," Kit Ternan was an exception. Milly saw in her a creative imagination, a fluidity in expressing herself in her compositions that was truly outstanding.

The fact that she had been "placed out" with the Hansen family gave Milly some concern. She had had Caspar and Lonny in her classes and denser, less teachable children would be rare to find. They seemed to have no intellectual stimulation at home and found their studies tedious and dull. The papers she returned to them were always full of red-penciled corrections, though she always suggested they "try harder next time."

Yet, Kit was special and Milly encouraged her writing. When she saw how Kit loved to read, she loaned her books from the school library as well as from her own personal collection.

If only Kit did not get bogged down by the chores Milly knew she was responsible for on the farm, did not get discouraged by the lack of intellectual stimulation in her environment. So far, neither of the Hansens had ever shown much interest in their own boys' education. Only once had Jess Hansen shown up, offering to "whup 'em good" when she had sent a note home with Lonny, complaining about his arithmetic sums.

Milly determined she herself would see that Kit's avid thirst for knowledge was nourished. The girl was too intelligent, and a mind was a terrible thing to waste!

Just then, Kit looked up and smiled at her, and Milly sensed that sweetness that always seemed to emanate from her, and smiled back.

How pretty Miss Cady is, thought Kit. *I want to be just like her when I grow up. I guess I'll be a teacher, too. When you're a teacher, you can read as many books as you want. You can live in a nice little cottage and have just flowers in your garden. You can wear frilly blouses, a fresh one every day, and combs in your hair and flowered hats on Sunday.*

Unconsciously Kit sighed. She had only been in Miss Cady's little house twice, and it was so different front the Hansens' farmhouse that she would like to have stayed forever. Miss Cady had offered to lend her some books and, even though Kit knew she would miss a ride home on the Wilsons' wagon and have to walk instead and probably be scolded for being late, it had been worth it. Miss Cady had let her pick out whichever two books she wanted. Kit had knelt for a long time in front of the bookcase in Miss Cady's parlor trying to make up her mind.

Afterwards they had had tea, real tea in pink china cups, sitting in front of a dear little polished stove. There was a plate of lemon circles stuck with cloves, and delicious wedges of thin cinnamon toast, all served on a small round table covered with a crisp linen cloth with a border of cross-stitch roses.

Kit's chest had seemed to swell with happiness so that it was almost hard to swallow. Everything about that afternoon stayed in her mind, like a picture she could take out and look at and enjoy all over again, times when she was lonely or life out at the Hansens was particularly dismal.

Kit bent her head over her workbook, her fingers tightening on her pencil. Maybe it wasn't right to wish such things, but, oh, how she wished she'd been "placed out" with Miss Cady. That was Kit's idea of pure heaven.

She bit her lip. Some days were really

hard. School was a welcome relief from the joyless routine on the farm. Kit got up before dawn to do her chores before it was time to walk down to the gate to get a ride into town with the Wilsons. Mr. Wilson went every day to do his milk deliveries and he would let his children and the Hansens off at the schoolyard.

Kit hated that ride. Of course, Lonny and Caspar either ran ahead or lagged behind her, making teasing jibes all the way. Then when they got on the back of the milk wagon, the Wilson girls, Susan and Ruby, were so mean. They had made it plain right from the start that they had no intention of making friends with her. The very first day of school they had drawn their pinafores away from Kit when she sat down beside them, put their noses in the air and sniffed, saying spitefully, "Orphan Trash!"

At least when she arrived at school, she had Laurel and Toddy, Kit thought gratefully.

Suddenly the school bell clanged and Kit and everyone jumped, looking up in surprise to see Miss Cady standing by the classroom door, a smile on her pretty face.

"Early dismissal today, boys and girls," she announced.

All the children scrambled to their feet, pencils dropped, workbooks slammed shut.

The room emptied as if by magic as everyone went running out. Only Kit remained. She came up to Milly's desk.

"Miss Cady, I wanted to ask you about the composition tablets," she began shyly. "I noticed most of them have a few pages left in them even though we've done our last essay for the year."

"Yes, what about them, Kit?" Milly asked.

"I wondered if I could go through them, tear out the blanks and have them?"

"I don't see why not. I was going to discard them anyway."

"Oh, thank you, Miss Cady. May I do it after school?"

"Certainly. But, I'm curious. Why do you want them?"

Kit lowered her eyes and color crept up into her cheeks. "I want to use them to write to my little brother and sister."

"Oh? I didn't realize you had a brother and sister, Kit. How old are they and where do they live?"

Kit shook her head. "I don't know. I mean, I know how old they are or how old they *must* be now. But I don't know where they are." She hesitated, then said slowly, "You see, they were adopted, and it's a secret where they're placed. But someday, when I'm a grown-up, I'm going to try to

65

find them. And in the meantime, I write them letters telling them about things, where I am, what I'm doing. I know how much Jamie, my brother, would love the farm. So I tell him things about the animals and all. And Gwynny, I'm afraid she will forget me, she was so little. So I write about things she wouldn't know about unless I told her. About our Da and our mother who Gwynny wouldn't remember at all —" Kit paused, her cheeks flushed, embarrassed that she had said so much. "That's what I write. That's why I want the paper."

Milly turned away, busying herself by erasing the blackboard. Her eyes stung. She felt like going to the teachers' supply cabinet and taking out a ream of fresh paper and giving it to Kit. But she knew that would further embarrass the child. So she went to the discard bin and took out an armful of used copybooks.

"If you'll wait a minute, Kit, I'll help you tear out the pages," was all she could trust herself to say.

Later, up in her room under the eaves, Kit read over some of the "letters" she had written over the past few months.

Dear Jamie and Gwynny,
    First, I'll tell you where I went after I

left Greystone. They put us on a train going West and it was very interesting and exciting as I've already written.

When we got to Meadowridge, I was placed out with a family who have a farm about three miles from town.

There is a barn and a big house. My room is on the top floor with a window where I can look out and see the whole farm — the fields, the orchards, the river, the pasture.

There are lots of different kinds of animals on the farm. In the pasture there are cows with lovely, soft velvety-brown eyes. There are a couple of workhorses Mr. Hansen uses to pull his plow and two more for the wagon when he goes into town. There are lots of chickens, and a cross old rooster who squawks and chases me every time I go out to feed them. But there are sweet, fluffy little baby chicks that Gwynny would love to pet.

Kit tried to describe all the good things about the farm she could think of, but there were things she didn't tell, things that made her sad even to think about. Like how the cows mourned when their calves were taken away to market.

The first time she had heard the pitiful

sound of loud mooing, she had rushed in to tell Cora that something must be dreadfully wrong with them. They must be sick or in pain. Cora matter-of-factly explained that they missed their calves.

"You mean like a mother would miss her baby?" asked Kit with tear-filled eyes.

Cora had given her a strange look, then nodded, her lips pressed together tightly.

Kit had crawled up in her bed, crying, too, as the mournful sound continued all the next day. She wondered if their Da ever missed *them* like that. But of course she didn't write that in her letters, either.

Sometimes what Kit wrote was more for herself than for her brother and sister. Some of her heart's deepest longings, her mind's most puzzling thoughts. After all, she wasn't at all sure Jamie and Gwynny would ever get to read the letters anyway.

The Hansen family has five boys. The two oldest, Caspar and Lonny, are terrible teases. I didn't think they liked me at all at first, but now I think it's just that they're boys and have to prove something. Still, I hope you'll never be that way, Jamie. The three younger ones are Seth, Chet, and Tom, who are turning out to be my friends.

When they had the measles and had to stay in bed with the curtains pulled, so the room would be dark and not damage their eyes, I read to them. Listening to the stories kept them quiet. I pretended I was reading to you and Gwynny. Anyhow, after they got well, they still wanted me to read to them. Mrs. Hansen says she hasn't time to do it.

But sometimes she'll have me sit in the kitchen, while she's making bread and read out loud to all of them. She says it keeps them out of mischief and from underfoot. But I think she likes the stories, too.

I wonder a lot about you two. Where did you go? Who adopted you? Are you happy? I daydream that one day we will find each other again, maybe not until we're all grown up.

I hope you haven't forgotten me.

Your loving sister,
Kit

Kit settled herself comfortably by the window, smoothing out the first copybook from the pile of used ones Miss Cady had given her, and began a new letter:

Dear Jamie and Gwynny,
School is nearly out for the year. Next

week we have report cards and Promotion. I got promoted to the Fifth Grade. I will have the same teacher, Miss Cady, the one I told you about because she teaches both Fourth and Fifth. She is so nice. I think I will be a teacher when I grow up, or maybe a writer —

9

The Class of 1900

Kit Ternan, at nearly nineteen, was a willowy brunette. Her hair, the color of polished maple, was swept back from her face, emphasizing her wide, gray eyes and lovely brow.

Her arms full of books, she came out of the main door of Meadowridge High School. Seeing groups of students who, lured by the warmth of the early June day, were sitting all over the steps, she paused at the top for a minute, wondering how to pick her way down through them.

Hearing the thunk of a tennis ball, she turned to look over at the school's tennis court where two couples were playing mixed doubles. She recognized her friends, Toddy and Laurel, at once. It was easy to guess who their partners were — Chris Blanchard and Dan Brooks.

Toddy sprinted toward the net, with the lightness of a butterfly, her blonde hair swinging like a silken bell from its bow glinted with golden lights in the sunshine.

Laurel, slender in her fashionable white tennis blouse and skirt, moved with graceful ease.

Kit moved to the other side of the porch for a better view and stood watching them. Laurel was poised with her racket at the base line, Toddy shifting her position in anticipation of Chris's serve. Dan's lean body crouched at the ready, twirled his racket waiting tensely for the play. A fast volley followed until Chris slammed a wicked backhand into the net, then raised both his hands and let out a frustrated howl. The others laughed and game was called. Still laughing the foursome walked toward the edge of the court.

Kit shifted her load of books, then threaded her way down the steps, stopping here and there to exchange a greeting as she did. As she went by the tennis court, Toddy saw her and waved.

"Wait, Kit!"

Leaving the others refreshing themselves at the water fountain, Toddy ran up to the wire-mesh door of the court, opened it, and came out.

"Can you?" Toddy asked. "Stay over with me after the Awards Banquet?"

Kit hesitated. "I haven't asked Cora yet. I will when I go out to the farm this weekend."

"She'll have to say yes. After all, it's part of Graduation Week," Toddy reminded her.

"I know, but we bake on Saturdays and she —"

"You can't miss the Awards Banquet, Kit!" Toddy protested. "Surely —"

"Oh, I won't miss it. It's just that staying over in town Friday night would put me late getting out to the farm Saturday morning and —"

"But it will be late when it's over and Laurel wants us all to come over to the Woodwards' house afterwards for our own party. You *must* stay over, Kit," Toddy insisted. "Do you want me to have Mrs. Hale write her a note, inviting you?"

Kit shook her head. "Cora hates getting notes. I'll ask her and explain. I think she'll understand —"

Toddy looked at her friend, for once her pert face serious. "You're over eighteen now, Kit. You know you don't have any further obligation to the Hansens. They haven't taken any responsibility for *you* since then, have they?" she demanded. "I mean, you *have* been living with Miss Cady this year."

Kit nodded, "I know. It's just that . . . well, Cora has so much to do, Toddy. You can't imagine what goes on every day at the farm.

With those five big boys there's so much cooking, baking and —"

"But you aren't their hired girl, Kit. If it hadn't been for Miss Cady, they might not have even let you finish high school!" Toddy sounded indignant.

"I think Cora would have, she wanted to, it was Jess — he just didn't, *doesn't* understand, that's all."

"Well, anyway, they haven't lifted a finger to help you finish your senior year and they're not doing anything to help you earn the money you'll need for college." Toddy paused and put on a severe expression. "They certainly aren't paying you for all the weekends you go out there and work, now are they?"

Kit shook her head. What Toddy was saying *was* true, but she felt disloyal admitting it. After all, the Hansens *had* given her a home all these years, fed, clothed her. So, instead of telling Toddy she was right, Kit changed the subject.

"Speaking of getting paid, I'd better run or I'll be late for work at the library and Miss Smedley will give me one of her famous lectures on a 'prompt and willing employee.'" Kit groaned.

"Looks like you're taking books back, not checking them out. I guess you've got the perfect after-school job for you."

"I know — 'bookworm,' that's me." Kit smiled, not annoyed by her friend's teasing.

"I should probably be at the library studying instead of playing tennis!" Toddy made a dismal face. "Two more final exams to get through."

Kit nodded sympathetically.

"Oh, *you* should worry, Kit. You'll pass with honors in everything. I'm the one who has to worry, especially about History. All those dates!" Toddy rolled her eyes.

Kit smiled. "Soon it will all be over and we'll be graduating."

"The Class of 1900! Just think!" Toddy grinned.

"I really have to go now, Toddy. I'll let you know about Friday," Kit promised as she set off down the shady street toward the town library.

On her way, Kit thought about what she and Toddy had discussed. Especially about Millicent Cady, who, ever since Kit was in her grammar school class, had taken such a special interest in her. Not only had she been Kit's ideal, she had been her mentor, guide and friend. It was Miss Cady who kept encouraging Kit to set goals, make plans, who fueled Kit's fire for learning.

"You've got a fine mind, Kit. It's God's

gift to you, so you must develop it and then you can share it with others," Miss Cady constantly told her. She urged Kit to apply for a scholarship to Merrivale Teachers College.

At first, that had sounded like an impossible dream. But, spurred on by Miss Cady's belief in her ability, Kit had pushed herself and worked hard so that her high-school marks were consistently excellent. This winter Miss Cady had helped her fill out the scholarship application. All that was needed now were her final exam grades. If she qualified, she would then go for a personal interview with the Dean of the Teacher's College. After that, she would just have to wait to see if she were accepted.

This had been the best of all her years in Meadowridge. But, if Miss Cady had not offered her a home, Kit might have had to quit school entirely.

Jess didn't set much store by "book larnin'," as he called it. Lonny and Caspar dropped out at Sixth Grade and now worked full time on the farm. Living there, Kit found it harder and harder to find time to study, do the required papers. The workload of chores — washing, cleaning, cooking, baking, sewing, mending — became heavier as the boys got older, bigger, hungrier and outgrew their clothes more rapidly.

Although Kit felt sorry for Cora, she knew if she stayed, she would be trapped. An existence that ignored the life of the intellect and spirit would be an imprisoning life for someone of Kit's sensitivity. She was indebted to Miss Cady, and each time she went back to the farm to help out, she realized more and more just how *much* she owed her.

Kit reached the old brick, ivy-covered library building, hurried up the steps, and went through the etched glass and wooden doors.

Once inside, Kit felt "at home." There was something familiar and comforting about the smell of paste, paper, old and new books, and the furniture wax that kept the golden oak tables and chairs gleaming. That was Amelia Smedley's doing. She felt she owned the public library after all the years she had worked here as head librarian. She took as much pride in its appearance as if it were her own home.

Ever since she had discovered it years before, the library was one of Kit's favorite places. She could still remember her sense of awe and wonder at first seeing shelf after shelf of books, learning they all could be taken out and read!

She still loved coming here, felt lucky to work here, even though Miss Smedley was considered a veritable "dragon" by most people.

As Kit slid her armload of books into the RETURN slot, Miss Smedley looked up from a pile of books she was cataloguing. Surveying Kit sternly over her pinch-nose glasses, she glanced at the wall clock. "You're late!"

Kit's eyes followed the glance, saw the minute hand jerk a little past four. Only three minutes late!

"Sorry, Miss Smedley."

Miss Smedley pointed with her stamper. "Get to work then."

Suppressing a smile, Kit went straight over to the book cart loaded with books to be shelved.

Kit looked out from the stacks where she was shelving books when the door opened and Dan Brooks walked into the library. Her hands started to shake so that she almost dropped the books she was holding. Her face flamed and her heart thundered.

That always happened when she saw Dan unexpectedly — coming toward her down a school corridor, or out on the school grounds, or walking along the sidewalk on the opposite side of the street in town, it didn't matter.

She was ashamed of the quick dart of envy she felt for Laurel, because she loved her friend dearly. But Laurel didn't even seem to notice Dan's worshipful attitude toward her. For some reason Laurel always seemed to have an air of detachment about her. It was almost as if she were a bird of passage, only temporarily among them.

It wasn't that Kit wished she could replace Laurel in Dan's affection exactly. It was just that her romance-starved heart secretly yearned for someone to gaze at her with such unconditional adoration. If it couldn't be Dan, then maybe someone just like him.

10

The day of the Senior Picnic, Kit, dressed in a crisp pink-checked gingham dress and swinging a wide-brimmed straw hat by its strings, walked from Miss Cady's cottage over to the high school feeling happier and more carefree than she could ever remember.

The blue sky, washed clear of clouds by a light rain that had fallen during the night, promised a perfect day ahead for the class outing. Even if it had been cloudy, nothing could have spoiled this day for Kit. Since yesterday, all of her dreams seemed possible.

Yesterday had been the last regular day of school in the last week before Graduation. Exams were over and, with most classes suspended, all the Seniors had to do was practice the processional and rehearse the songs they were to sing at the program.

The Seniors had filed into the auditorium for morning assembly with more than the usual amount of chatter. An undercurrent of excitement buzzed among them.

Mr. Henson, the principal, standing at the

lectern on the stage, had to rap more times than usual for things to quiet down enough so he could be heard.

"Students, your attention, please. Before I dismiss the rest of you except for the Seniors, who have to rehearse for Graduation, I want to make the announcement I'm sure you have all been waiting to hear — the names of the Seniors who will represent the Class of 1900 as Salutatorian and Valedictorian."

A murmur of anticipation rippled through the room.

"Actually there was very little difference in the grade point averages of the two top students. The Salutatorian, as you know, makes the welcoming speech. The Valedictorian will give the speech summing up the feelings, thoughts, future goals of our departing Senior Class."

Mr. Henson cleared his throat, adjusted his spectacles and, referring to the paper he held, said, "This year's Salutatorian of Meadowridge High's graduating class, we are proud to name — Daniel Brooks."

Kit's hands became clammy as the announcement hit her like a blow, knocking the breath out of her. Only the evening before, Miss Cady had confided excitedly that when she had gone into the high-school office on some pretext, she had seen some of the Senior grades.

"Yours were very high, Kit! You have a very good chance of being named Salutatorian even though a girl has never spoken at Graduation before."

Just that morning before Kit left for school, Miss Cady had hugged her impulsively. "I just know you'll be named Salutatorian, Kit. And now there'll be no question of your getting a scholarship to Merrivale," she assured her.

Kit fought back tears, battled her disappointment while all around her their classmates began applauding as Dan stumbled to his feet, looking both bewildered and pleased.

Kit started clapping, too. Of course, it would be Dan, she told herself. Dan was outstanding, intelligent, a brilliant student. He deserved it. It had been foolish to hope. Kit clapped harder so that her palms stung.

Mr. Henson let the clapping go on for nearly a full minute before holding up his hand for silence.

"And now, for a precedent-setting announcement, which seems particularly fitting for the first class graduating in the beginning of a new century. After tabulating the grades repeatedly to be sure there was no possible mistake, we have come to the conclusion that this year's Valedictorian will for the first time be a young woman — Miss Kathleen Ternan."

Kit had sat there, completely motionless, her hands pressed against her mouth, while pandemonium broke all about her. She heard a roaring in her ears as her heart thundered, beating in her chest as if it might explode.

It couldn't be happening! Had she really heard it right? Had Mr. Henson announced her name?

"Kit! Kit!" Someone was tugging her arm. "Mr. Henson wants you to come up on the stage."

It was Toddy and, on the other side, Laurel was hugging her. The sound of applause rose in crescendo as Kit somehow managed to get to the end of the row and make her way up the steps of the stage. As she reached its center, Mr. Henson was holding out his hand to shake hers, and Dan, standing alongside the principal, was grinning and clapping like the rest.

Kit turned toward the assembly and, through happy tears, she saw that all the student body had risen in a standing ovation.

Yes, yesterday had probably been the happiest day of her life. If only Da could have known and Jamie and Gwynny could have seen their big sister receive such an honor! Of course, Toddy and Laurel had been thrilled, treated her to a soda at Shay's Ice Cream Parlor after school to celebrate. But it would have been nice to have *real* family there.

In sight of the schoolyard now, Kit was hailed by some of the other Seniors arriving for their class picnic. Kit was admired and well-liked by her classmates, and several of the Senior boys would have been eager to claim her as a girl friend. However, Kit never had any time for anything but school and her work at the library. Her weekends were spent out at the Hansens' farm, helping Cora.

Some of the more enterprising fellows who ordinarily did not care much for extra reading frequented the library, hoping Kit would be checking out books that evening.

Although Kit did not have Laurel's "candy-box" prettiness nor Toddy's gamine appeal, she was attractive. Today the sun gave her rich brown hair a golden sheen, and her clear skin had a becoming apricot glow. But her eyes were her best feature — large, beautiful, a silvery gray set in thick, dark lashes.

Today, Kit was so filled with joy that she radiated happiness and her fellow classmates felt drawn to her in a new and special way. Everyone wanted to sit with her as they climbed into the wagons filled with hay to ride out to River Park, sit beside her on the rustic benches at the tables in the park where a lavish picnic was set out.

But it was with Toddy and Laurel that Kit always felt most at ease. Wherever those two were, Chris Blanchard and Dan Brooks could usually be found. After lunch the five friends left the picnic area to climb up the hill leading to the bluff overlooking the river.

"Written your speech yet, Kit?" Dan asked in mock seriousness.

"Of course! A hundred times, haven't you?" she laughed in return.

"I'm so proud of you two!" declared Toddy. "Imagine being friends with two celebrities!"

"Are you going to be a suffragette, Kit?" asked Chris. "Votes for women and all that sort of thing?"

"She'll probably end up being the first woman President of the United States," Toddy told him as they reached the top.

Kit stretched flat on her back, tilted the broad-brimmed straw hat over her face. Her hands at her sides stroked the grass on which she lay. She breathed deeply, as if she could take everything — the sun, the scents, the cloudless sky — into her very being, wanting to hold onto it forever.

The thought drifted through her mind to try, because instinctively she knew it was the kind of day to be looked back upon and remembered at some distant time.

Kit heard the voices, muted laughter coming up from the river where Chris and Toddy were skipping rocks across its sun-sparkled surface. She heard Laurel softly humming some melody. She wondered if any of them were as aware as she of the swift passage of time. This week they would graduate from high school and then everything would change. She wanted to cry out to them, but what would she have said? They would have thought her ridiculous if she had stood up and shouted, "Behold! This, too, shall pass."

Kit smiled to herself. Yes, they would have thought her mad. But her own awareness gripped her in an urgent need to savor this day.

"Penny for your thoughts, Kit!" Dan interrupted her reverie.

Would Dan understand if she shared them with him? Maybe. But not being sure, she raised herself on her elbows, pushed back the brim of her hat, smiled over at both him and Laurel, and quoted softly from one of the poems in the book of collected verse of Elizabeth Barrett Browning Miss Cady had given her.

> The little cares that fretted me.
> I lost them yesterday
> Among the fields above the sea,
> Among the winds at play,
> Among the lowing of the herds,
> The rustling of the trees,
> Among the singing of the birds,
> The humming of the bees,
> The foolish fears of what may happen.
> I cast them all away.
> Among the clover-scented grass,
> Among the new-mown hay:
> Among the husking of the corn,
> Where drowsy poppies nod,
> Where ill thoughts die and good are born —
> Out in the fields with God!

"That's beautiful, Kit." Toddy's voice was enthusiastic as she and Chris reappeared. "Will you write that down for me, please? Mr. Allen asked me to find something appropriate to recite at the Baccalaureate Breakfast, and that would be perfect."

"Sure," agreed Kit.

Just then they heard the shrill sound of a

whistle, the teachers' signal to come to the main picnic area for the ride back to town. Reluctantly, they began to straggle back down the hillside.

Kit was the last to leave. She stopped, and looked back. The sun's rays were beginning to touch the hills, sending long, purple shadows across the waving meadow grass. She had the feeling of saying goodbye to something precious. To what? Youth? Freedom? Or only a perfect day?

She had to smile at her own dramatizing. Surely there would be other days when the five of them would come back to this hill during the coming summer. But she knew it would never be quite the same as this one idyllic day. For some reason Kit shivered and hurried after the others.

11

Hairbrush in hand, Kit studied her reflection in the mirror and frowned. Her arms were weary from practicing doing up her hair as she wanted to wear it for Graduation. It was much too thick and heavy to pouf up in front, combing it over the wire "rats" some girls used to achieve the popular pompadour style. So she had brushed it to a satiny sheen, braided it, and turned it under at the nape of her neck, securing it with tortoise shell hairpins.

This style was not in fashion, she knew, but it was all she could manage and looked well enough, she decided. Even if her hairdo did not satisfy her, Kit felt pleased and happy with her graduation outfit. The white tucked blouse was simple but dainty, and the white skirt fit her slim figure perfectly.

Miss Cady had suggested that she buy a good quality material for a skirt, then make two blouses. That way she had had two outfits to wear to the events. Miss Cady had given her the lace for the blouse — *real* lace! Miss Cady said a lady *never* wore *machine-*

made lace. Of course Kit would not have known that unless Miss Cady had gently told her. The lace simply *made* her blouse.

Yes, Miss Cady was right as she was about all the fine points of being a lady. "Understatement" was so much more in good taste than the flamboyant patterns and fabric the clerk at Donninger's Dry Goods had tried to sell her.

"Half the girls in the graduating class will go for that sort of thing," Miss Cady told Kit. "But you will stand out in your elegant simplicity. People will see *you,* not what you're wearing. They'll remember your words, not your dress. And, after all, that's the important thing. You will be the first female Valedictorian Meadowridge High has ever had! Just think, Kit!"

Miss Cady had gone to her weekly Wednesday Night Prayer Meeting, and Kit was alone. She was giving her blouse and skirt a final careful pressing in the kitchen when the front doorbell rang. She set the iron on its heel, then slipped her blouse off the ironing board, hung it on a hanger, hooked it over the doorknob, then ran to answer the door. Maybe Miss Cady had forgotten her key.

To her surprise, it was Cora.

"I almost left, thought nobody was home,"

Cora said. "I wuz just goin' to leave this, but now I see you're here, I'll jest bring it on in myself and see you open it." She bent down and picked up a large cardboard box she had propped beside the front door and, as Kit held the door open wider, Cora squeezed in carrying it.

"There now!" Cora let out her breath as she put the box down. "Where's your bedroom, Kit?"

Kit realized Cora had never been to Miss Cady's cottage before. Still astonished by this unexpected visit, she led the way down the short hall to her room.

"This doesn't mean you're not coming tomorrow, does it?" Kit asked, turning to Cora with a worried frown.

"Oh, no, we're comin' all right. But I jest come in myself to bring you this." Cora laid the box on Kit's bed. Then she stood back, hands on her hips, and pointed to the box. "Well, go ahead. Don't you want to see what's inside?" Her thin lips twitched a little.

Still puzzled, Kit undid the string tied around the box and lifted off the lid. Then she pushed aside the tissue paper on top. A wave of dismay washed over her when she saw the contents.

"Oh, Cora, you shouldn't have!"

"Well, aren't you goin' to take it out, try it on?" prodded Cora, hardly able to contain her own excitement.

Kit reached in and slowly unfolded the most impossible dress she could have imagined. At the same time, she knew Cora thought it the most beautiful.

"I thought you should have a store-bought dress for once, Kit. So I ordered it out of that mail-order catalog from Chicago. They have the latest fashions, you know," Cora said, reaching out to touch the gleaming sateen surface of the tiered skirt trimmed with row after row of *machine-made* lace.

Unable to speak, Kit held the dress up to herself, turning away so Cora could not see her face betray her true feelings about this disaster of a dress.

The leg-of-mutton sleeves were ribboned to the elbow, the cuffs banded with the same lace as the skirt and bodice. For a minute Kit closed her eyes and prayed desperately for the right words to say.

Cora, her head to one side, was surveying the dress from behind.

"You'll have to slip it on with the shoes you'll be wearin' so's we can see if the length is right. We still have time to take up the hem if needs be."

Speechless, Kit got out of her cotton skirt and shirtwaist, and stood in her camisole and petticoat while Cora, humming under her breath, dropped the dress over Kit's head and proceeded to do up the buttons in the back.

"Well now, I think it's goin' to fit just fine," Cora said with satisfaction.

Kit, who had hoped against hope that it would be too big or too tight, suppressed a groan of despair. She dreaded looking in the mirror. She could only imagine how wrong in every way this awful dress was.

"There now, Kit, what do you think?" asked Cora.

It was the ultimate test. It took Kit only a second to conquer her own self-will, the length of a whispered prayer. Then she turned around and gave Cora a hug. "Oh, Cora, thank you! It was such a thoughtful thing for you to do. I just can't tell you how much I appreciate your doing it." All the words were true but every one cost Kit dearly.

"Well, no need to make such a fuss." Cora pulled away self-consciously. "I just didn't want you up on that platform lookin' dowdy beside the doctor's girl and that sassy little baggage from the Hale's." She took a step back and surveyed Kit again. "If I do say so myself, not another girl graduatin' will hold a candle to you in *that*." She pursed her lips, which was Cora's way of showing she was pleased. "Well, I best be goin' if I'm to get home afore dark. I was waitin' and waitin' for this to come. Don't know how many trips I made to the Post Office to see if it had got here yet," she exclaimed with a shake of her head. "T'would've been a real pity if you hadn't had it to wear fer your Graduation."

Oh, if only it *hadn't* come, thought Kit miserably.

She walked to the door with Cora, stood there and watched Cora climb into the wagon and drive off. Then she shut the door and leaned against it, her head pressed on the wood, wanting to bang it in frustration.

Of all the years, of all the times she might have been thrilled that Cora thought enough of her to spend the money to order her a dress, *why now?* When it didn't matter, or rather, when it mattered *so much.*

Kit walked slowly back into the bedroom and stared at her reflection in the mirror. The material felt sleazy against her skin, the cheap lace scratched her chin and wrists. Her face crumpled. She *hated* this dress! She looked — like an over dressed, over frilled — floozy! Kit slid to her knees, buried her face in her hands as bitter tears forced themselves up through her throat and broke out in hoarse sobs.

The occasion when she had planned to look her very best, when she would be standing in front of all Meadowridge to give the Valedictory speech she had worked so long and hard over, was ruined for her.

Finally she wiped her tears. Sighing heavily, she got to her feet, stumbling a little over the ruffled hem. As she did, her eyes caught sight of the white blouse with its dainty real lace on its hanger on the doorknob, and a new wave of despair swept over her. Kit thought of the hours she had spent sewing it, laboring over its tiny tucks and delicate stitches. All wasted time now.

There was no way out. She would *have* to wear the dress Cora had chosen for her. Kit could imagine how she must have sat at the kitchen table in the light of the oil lamp, poring over the pages of the huge mail-order catalog. How she must have got Lonny or Caspar, no, probably Seth, to print out the order for her, address, and mail it. And that would have taken some humbling for Cora to do, Kit knew. When Kit had been at the Hansens' less than a year, she had discovered Cora's shameful secret, the one she kept well hidden. Cora could not read or write.

She understood what a gift of love this was from Cora, even if it was tinged with self-pride and the oft-revealed resentment she had toward the other Orphan Train adoptive homes. It was a gift Kit must receive with gracious gratitude, no matter what.

As Kit started to unbutton the dress, she heard the front door open and Miss Cady's light step coming down the hall.

"Kit, are you still up? Did you realize you left the lamp lighted in the kitchen and the ironing board up?" Miss Cady stopped at her half-open bedroom door.

"What on earth are you doing in that dreadful dress?" she asked with undisguised horror.

Kit lifted her chin, straightened her shoulders. "Cora brought it to me. It's for Graduation."

"To wear? On Graduation Day? You can't possibly wear it, Kit, dear. It's perfectly awful!"

Kit's clear, gray eyes regarded her with uncompromising directness. "I have to, Miss Cady," she said firmly. "I'm going to."

12

Graduation Day was as beautiful a June day as one could wish and, as the Seniors filed into the auditorium, they looked suitably solemn and grown up for this occasion. Some of the girls had their hair up for the first time, and the boys, looking a little uncomfortable, were still smart in their unaccustomed stiff-collared shirts, ties, and dark suits.

The hall was full. High school graduation in Meadowridge was an important event since only a few graduates went on to college. This, then, was a special milestone in their lives, the point where they officially stepped into the responsibilities of adulthood. Family and friends had gathered to witness this transition.

As the day warmed outside, so did the interior. Palmetto fans made a rhythmic crackling sound as they were wafted to and fro.

After the singing of the school song, a prayer was offered by Reverend Brewster. Then a few congratulatory words to the graduates were made by Mayor Clinton.

Finally, Mr. Henson, the Principal, got up and patting his perspiring bald forehead, first spoke directly to the graduates.

"Many of you may remember being called into my office at some time in the past four years for something or other. Be it a serious matter or less so, I would like to say whatever the reason, it was because I cared for each of you and was deeply interested in you individually. I wanted you to leave Meadowridge High with everything you needed to utilize in your lives thereafter.

"It has been a fine four years. As a class you have been a real asset to our school, and I wish you all well in whatever endeavors you undertake.

"So, on behalf of all the teachers and staff, to each and every Graduate, our best wishes and sincere hope that as you move into the Twentieth Century, you will take with you the highest ideals, the noblest purposes, the purest goals and will each make an individual contribution to the betterment of society, and the world."

Directing his remaining words to the rest of the audience he said, "We have only set them on their paths, equipped them with a sound education, tried to give them the foundations, exposed them to a faith that should strengthen them. We wish them all well on the journey on which they are about to embark, to develop their talents, fulfill their destinies."

The applause was generous and would have lasted longer if Mr. Henson had not held up his hands to halt it.

"Thank you all, but we want to give these young people their chance. First, I give you the Salutatorian of the Class of 1900, Mr. Daniel Brooks."

Dan stepped up to the podium, cleared his throat and began. His voice was husky and low. "Welcome, honored guests, families and friends. We, the Class of 1900, are all well aware of the significance of leaving high school in the dawning year of a new century."

Kit, knowing she had her own speech to give after Dan's, controlled her nervousness by making herself concentrate on every word he was saying. In spite of her intention, it was Dan himself who occupied her thoughts. She saw his body taut with tension leaning on the podium, his hands gripping the sides, and she whispered a little prayer to calm him. She admired the set of his head with its sandy thickness slicked down for this occasion, the profile that would one day be considered distinguished but was still painfully boyish — the nose a little too long, the chin a bit too prominent. But to Kit, Dan was very handsome, had always been.

He would be leaving at the end of the summer to start his medical training, and she, thanks to her scholarship, would be going to Merrivale Teachers College. When would they see each other again?

Unconsciously Kit's eyes moved over to Laurel's cameo-perfect profile, and felt ashamed of the prick of envy she felt for her friend. Laurel was so cherished by the Woodwards. Everything seemed to come to her so easily, especially love. She hardly seemed conscious of Dan's. But Laurel took it all for granted, as if everyone should love her and be loved in return, while for Kit —

Kit pulled herself back to the moment, heard Dan saying something about the "wide path full of opportunities that lies ahead for each of us," and realized that the path ahead of her would be a lonely one, one she must take by herself, with no one to depend on. If only there were someone like Dan to *care,* to hold her hand, to at least walk along beside her, Kit thought wistfully.

No self-pity, she warned herself. Actually, she was terribly lucky. A full four-year scholarship and Miss Cady so willing to help her — It was wrong to envy anyone, to wish things were different.

Hearing Dan's words, "In closing," Kit jerked herself back from her daydreams to listen to his finish.

"May I recite the immortal lines written by the great American poet Henry Wadsworth Longfellow, words it would be well worth our while to take as our talisman and to inspire us as we start out in the great adventure of life." Dan's voice deepened dramatically as he quoted: "Lives of great men all remind us/ We can make our lives sublime/ And departing leave behind us/ Footprints in the sands of time./ Let us then be up and doing/ With a heart for any fate/ Still achieving, still pursuing/ Learn to labour and to wait."

Kit felt her throat swell with emotion. How could her own speech equal Dan's flowing rhetoric, the high-sounding phrases, the call to nobility? In comparison, hers seemed ambitious and self-serving. But there was no chance now to change it. Soon, the diplomas would be given out and she would be called up to the podium to speak.

Cora raised her chin, looking over the heads of the people seated in the row in front of her, and observed Kit with pride.

If Kit don't look better'n any of them, she thought to herself with satisfaction. Don't care a bit that Jess ranted and raved over my gettin' that dress for the girl. Was my egg money anyhow, weren't it? I wasn't about to let that snippy Miss Cady or the doctor's wife or that high and mighty Miz Hale think we didn't do right by Kit. After all, it was us who took her in, sent her to school all these years, except for this last one. If it hadn't been for us, she might not have even got to high school. Some of the Orphan Train kids placed out on farms had to quit school after the Eighth Grade and work full-time on the fields or in the house. That's what Jess thought Kit oughta do. But I stood up to him. I knew Kit was bright, brighter than most, and she oughta have her chance.

She's been a good girl all these years. Couldn't ask for anyone more willin' to lend a hand. She's taken a load off me, that's fer shure. Come right down to it, I'd have been hard put to keep things up if it waren't fer Kit's help. 'Specially with my back and side givin' me fits so much of the time. And Kit seemed to know when I was feelin' poorly. I never had to say a word. She'd just take over, push me into my room, and tell me to sit a spell. She put up over twenty quarts of berries, canned those peaches, and made applesauce this past fall all by herself. Of course, Seth turned to and give her a hand.

Seth really liked Kit. Always did from when she first came. She's helped him with his schoolwork and he's bright, too. Wisht Jess'd see that, and let him keep on in school for a little time longer. But he won't. Not worth talkin' or thinkin' about. Another hand in the field is what Jess wants. If he buys another six acres, he'll need Seth then. Well, since this is probably the only high school Graduation I'll ever go to, I better stop my mind wandering and pay attention to what's goin' on. After all, Kit's going to make a speech.

Yes, I'm sure glad I got her that dress. She looks real fine. I 'spect Miz Woodward and Miz Hale are takin' note of it.

Moonlight streamed through the dimity curtains of Kit's bedroom, making pale squares on the floor. She sat at the window, taking her hairpins out one by one, letting her heavy hair drop over her shoulders. She drew her brush slowly through its silky length. Under her breath she softly hummed the melody of the music she had danced to with Dan.

Graduation had been splendid. Kit had floated all through the day on a kind of suspended cloud. Even having to wear the awful dress seemed unimportant in the overall loveliness of the day. And tonight, had been — practically perfect.

A sigh escaped as Kit allowed herself the luxury of remembering the magical evening. Her mind relived that moment when the band had stopped playing and she had found herself standing opposite Dan in the Paul Jones. To be honest, she had seen a slight expression of disappointment cross Dan's face when he saw Laurel standing next to Kit, only a step away from becoming his partner for the next set. Then he had smiled his warm, pleasant smile and held out his hand to Kit to lead her into the lilting rhythm of the music.

Kit knew all her secret dreams about Dan were foolish. He had never been interested in any other girl but Laurel. Much as she might want to see in Dan's eyes the spark that flared when his gaze was on Laurel, Kit knew it was a futile hope.

They were friends and that was all they would ever be. And Laurel was her friend, too. A dear friend, just as Toddy was. The three of them were bonded by all the things that had happened to them, what they had survived and what was known only to each other. She did not want to covet anything Laurel had. Even Dan's love.

A solitary tear rolled down Kit's face, and

she brushed it away impatiently. This was not the night for tears. The summer ahead was going to be a busy one, a summer to work hard, prepare for the fall when she would be going away to Merrivale.

In spite of her longings, Kit knew it was not the right time for romantic fantasies. She had exciting ambitions, plans for the future she must strive to achieve. And then there was her long-held, cherished goal that somehow, some way, someday, she was going to find Jamie and Gwynny. There had always been that empty place in her heart for her little brother and sister.

Kit had no idea how she would go about it, where she would start, how she would trace them. But she knew she was going to, knew she must. It was a promise she had made to herself long ago, one she meant to keep.

13

Laurel was waiting outside the library when Kit got off work at four o'clock.

"Come over for a visit." Laurel begged, slipping her arm through Kit's. "I'm longing to talk to you. I've hardly seen you since Graduation and I have so much to discuss with you."

Kit hesitated slightly. The secret locked in her heart created a barrier between her and her friend, even though Laurel could not possibly know. It bothered Kit that she could not be as open with Laurel as she had always been before, and she longed for the old uncomplicated friendship they had always known.

"You can, can't you, Kit? There's no reason why not, is there?"

"No, I s'pose not," Kit replied, and Laurel gave her arm a little squeeze.

"Good! Papa Lee has taken Mother for a drive in the country so we'll have the whole house to ourselves. I have heaps to tell you."

Kit hoped it wasn't news about Dan. She dreaded hearing Laurel say that she and Dan had exchanged promises about the future. Kit wasn't sure how she could hear that and not betray her own feelings.

When they reached the Woodward house, Laurel stopped in the empty kitchen to fill two glasses with lemonade from a pitcher kept cool in the icebox on the back porch, then placed several thin molasses cookies from a jar on the counter, on a plate, and put everything on a tray for them to carry upstairs to her bedroom.

"Now, isn't this nice?" Laurel asked, smiling as they settled themselves on the window seat that circled the bay window overlooking the garden. "We'll have some privacy for a change."

Sipping the tangy lemonade, Kit's eyes circled the room thoughtfully. The late afternoon sun touched the maple wood bureau and the high spool bed with a golden polish, gave an added luster to the rosy-glass globe of the lamp on the desk, brightened the color of the climbing roses on the trellised wallpaper.

"Oh, Kit, I've been absolutely dying to confide in someone! I think I will burst if I don't tell!" Laurel exclaimed breathlessly. Her eyes were shining, and Kit's heart sank. Surely Laurel was planning to tell her she was in love with Dan! Unconsciously, Kit drew back as if to shield herself from a coming blow.

"And I knew it had to be *you*, Kit. Because, well, actually you're sort of responsible for it."

"Me? How? What am I responsible for?" gasped Kit.

"My decision." Laurel leaned closer. "Kit, I've decided to go away from Meadowridge to study voice! Mr. Fordyce approves, I mean, he told me if I were to go on, that is develop my singing so that I could, perhaps, well, I'm not sure exactly what I will do with it — but he said, I must go to a Conservatory for further training."

Kit's surprise rendered her speechless.

"Yes, I know what you're thinking!" Laurel rushed on. "But wait until I tell you *where* I plan to go! To Boston! There's a famous Music Conservatory there, and besides, remember *Greystone* is in Massachusetts." Laurel lowered her voice conspiratorially. "I plan to go there, look up my records and then — Kit, I am going to try to find my mother's family!"

With that, Laurel sat back and waited for Kit's reaction. When it did not come immediately, she demanded, "So, what do you think of *that?*"

Kit's clear, gray eyes under the dark, level

brows regarded her with unflinching honesty. "I'm wondering what the *Woodwards* think of it," she replied.

A momentary shadow crossed Laurel's face.

"Oh, they don't know yet. I haven't told them."

Again Kit's glance traveled the perfectly appointed room — the flowered carpet, the bookcase stocked with all the classics, the ceiling-high armoire stuffed with Laurel's lovely clothes. Laurel was so cherished by the Woodwards. They had made life easy for her, their love evident in every detail of this room planned for her comfort and enjoyment.

As the silence lengthened between them, Laurel said quickly, "Oh, but I'm going to, of course. I intend to. I'm just waiting for the right time."

Instinctively Kit's eyebrows lifted. Would there ever be a right time for Laurel to tell the Woodwards she was leaving? Leaving all this they had provided for her?

"You haven't said what you think, Kit. Don't you see I'm only doing what you urged us all to do in your Valedictory speech?"

Kit took a deep breath. My *speech?* The words she had written and memorized and spoken only a few short weeks ago repeated themselves now in her mind.

"We are all individuals, let us not be poor imitations of anyone, no matter how much we admire them. Let us light our own torches, carry our own standards, fly our own flags. No one has ever said it better than Shakespeare in *Hamlet*, 'This above all, to thine own self be true, And it must follow, as the night the day, Thou canst not then be false to any man.' "

Laurel's voice brought her back to the moment.

"So you see, Kit. I'm being true to myself — the real self, the one before Greystone or Meadowridge or the Woodwards. I have a family, a history that belongs to *me* and I've got to find it, don't you understand?"

"But, Laurel, you have everything *here!*" protested Kit softly, comparing Laurel's situation to the one she had had all these years with the Hansens. It had only been a matter of chance — two little orphan girls coming to the same town, two families. Laurel had gone to the Woodwards, Kit to the Hansens — Kit threw out both hands in an encompassing gesture, looking about her in puzzled amazement. "How can you leave all this? People who love and care about you, this — ?"

"*You're* going away!" Laurel accused. "You're being true to yourself, aren't you?"

"But that's not the same. I'm not leaving anything like this, Laurel. I'm hoping to find something better. Could anything be better than all this?"

"Don't you *really* understand, Kit?" Laurel asked again. "Don't you *really know?* Nothing ever makes up for being an orphan."

Just then they heard the sound of carriage wheels below, and glancing out the window, they saw Dr. Woodward's buggy turn into the driveway. In another minute Mrs. Woodward was calling up the stairs.

"Laurel, darling, are you up there? We're home!"

Kit left soon after in spite of Ava Woodward's gracious invitation to stay for supper. As she walked over to Miss Cady's cottage, Kit's mind was filled with what Laurel had confided in her.

The strangest thing of all was that Laurel had never even mentioned Dan. Did he know her plans? Or would he, too, be told when the "time was right"? Did that mean Laurel did not have any serious feelings for him? Kit was sure Dan loved Laurel. She had seen it in his eyes every time he looked at her. Kit's heart ached for him if Laurel did not return his love. Kit knew too well that kind of pain.

Poor Dr. and Mrs. Woodward. They would be lost without Laurel, who was the center of their lives. But, in a way, Kit *did* understand Laurel's need to leave. There had been times when she had felt the cloying, claustrophobic atmosphere with which the Woodwards surrounded Laurel. With all the best intentions, they had, perhaps, kept Laurel too sheltered, kept her on too tight a string pulled by two kind, but overly protective people.

It was a crippling kind of love. Like a bird whose wings had been clipped to keep it safely within the bounds of an enclosed aviary.

Kit was torn between sympathy for the Woodwards, who would be devastated when they learned of Laurel's plans, and admiration for Laurel, ready to give up all she had to strike out on her own.

Underneath, Kit concluded, all three of them — the Orphan Train trio — were the same. They were all somehow incomplete. There was an emptiness in each of them they longed to fill, even if it was just *knowing* the truth of why they had come to be at Greystone and then put on the Orphan Train, and "placed out." It didn't seem to matter *where* that had been. Just like Laurel had said, "Nothing ever makes up for being an orphan."

14

Kit was packing her trunk. Tomorrow she would be leaving for Merrivale Teachers College. She still almost had to pinch herself to believe it, even though she had received her registration forms, been given her dormitory room assignment as well as the name of her roommate. A Maude Lytle from Myrtle Creek.

She hummed as she laid the five neatly ironed shirtwaists on the top layer of the trunk — two plain white, one blue chambray with white collars and cuffs, a dark blue and green plaid one. She had three skirts — a gray wool, a brown and gold plaid, a black one for Sundays. Miss Cady had given her a lovely, soft knitted coat sweater and matching tam. Mrs. Woodward had gifted her with an elegant teal blue jacket and skirt for very best. She had a half-dozen chemises, camisoles, petticoats as well, stockings and two pairs of shoes — sturdy boots for every day, and high-buttoned black ones with a nice heel for Sundays and any other dress-up occasions there might be.

The school brochure, now worn on the edges from repeated readings, stated: "Merrivale students have many opportunities to attend concerts, plays and other cultural events."

Kit gave a rapturous sigh and twirled around her bedroom a couple of times. As Miss Cady kept saying, it would be a "glorious adventure," as she recalled her own college days.

For the dozenth time Kit checked her train ticket, her purse in which the hard-earned money from her summer job was safely stowed. How could she possibly live through the next few days until she was actually on her way?

The sound of insistent knocking on the front door interrupted Kit's happy occupation and she started down the hall to the front door to answer it. But Miss Cady must have heard it first because she heard her say, "Why, Lonny Hansen, what on earth brings you all the way into town this late in the evening?"

" 'Evenin', Miss Cady. Is Kit here?"

"Yes, she is, but what do you want with her?"

"Please, miss, I got to speak to her —"

By this time Kit was standing in the hall behind Miss Cady. Lonny's face looked ghastly pale, the freckles standing out in sharp relief against the unusual pallor of his skin.

"What is it, Lonny?" Kit asked, something in the back of her brain flashing a warning signal.

"Ma's ben took bad, Kit. Doc Woodward's out there now. My pa wants to know if you'll come?"

"What happened, an accident?" Kit asked with stiff lips.

"Some kind of spell. Pa and me found her when we come in from the field. Laid out on the kitchen floor, she were. Eyes all rolled back, hardly breathin', all stiff-like. Pa sent Caspar for the doctor. Then he and me carried her into bed. Her face is all twisted, she can't talk. I dunno, Kit. But can you come?"

Miss Cady turned to Kit. "But of course, you can't go out there now. You're leaving tomorrow! Surely Dr. Woodward can get a district nurse to help out —"

"Kit, I've got the wagon out front," Lonny said, his voice squeaky. "Pa said to ask you to hurry —"

"Lonny, you'll have to tell your father to get someone else. One of the women on the neighboring farm. Surely he can't expect Kit —"

"No, Miss Cady, I have to go," Kit's voice

116

rang out, interrupting her. To Lonny she spoke calmly. "I'll come, Lonny. Just a few minutes till I get some things."

"I'll wait in the wagon. But hurry, Kit, Ma's . . . well, she's awful sick."

Kit turned and ran back to her bedroom, pulled out her old, battered suitcase from under the bed, and started throwing a few things into it — her hairbrush, nightgown and wrapper.

"Kit, you can't do this. You can't go!" Miss Cady's voice spoke sharply. She had followed Kit and now stood in the doorway.

"Don't you see I have to go?" Kit pleaded. "There is nothing else I *can* do. Cora's done so much for me —"

"Done so much?" Miss Cady's voice rose, her face contorting angrily. "What have they done? Allowed you to do all the menial chores, let you sleep in their attic, be their unpaid slavey all these years? Come to your senses, Kit. You don't owe the Hansens a thing. Or if you ever did, it's been paid a hundred times over."

Kit pressed her lips together but didn't answer.

"Kit, are you listening? Do you hear what I'm saying?"

"Yes, Miss Cady, I do," she replied, folding her blouse and putting it in the suitcase.

She shook her head. "I do, but I have to go. You heard what Lonny said, how desperate he looked —"

"Then let that old skinflint, Jess Hansen, pay somebody to come and nurse his wife. It's not up to *you, Kit!* You're on the brink of a whole new wonderful life. You *can't* give that up. If you don't take it, they'll give the scholarship to someone else and who knows if you can get another one."

Kit hung her head, tears gathered stingingly in her eyes. Why couldn't Miss Cady help her? Didn't she see how hard this was? Her hands shook as she closed the lid of her suitcase and snapped the latches.

"I have to go now, Miss Cady. Lonny's waiting."

Miss Cady felt the blood surge into her head, her temples throbbed and her throat hurt as she rasped out the words, "I can't believe you're throwing away everything you worked so hard for. Everything *I* worked to help you achieve! Who knows how long Cora Hansen will live? She may go like that." She snapped her fingers. "Or she might linger for weeks, months, even years! And you'll be trapped. It's not your responsibility, Kit!"

But Kit was already at the door, her hand on the knob.

"I'm sorry, Miss Cady, sorry to disappoint you, but I have to go."

Miss Cady lost control then.

"How can you do this? How can you be so unappreciative, after all I've done to bring you this far? I've devoted years to you because I thought you were worth it, and now you're giving it all up!"

Kit's back was to her, but Miss Cady saw the slender shoulders stiffen. Then she opened the door and went out.

For a stunned moment Miss Cady watched the slim straight figure go down the cottage steps out to the waiting wagon. Then she heard herself scream.

"Kit, you'll be sorry! You'll never have another chance like this!"

Kit was climbing up into the wagon. As Miss Cady's voice reached her, she stared straight ahead, willing herself not to give way entirely to the despair and sadness churning within. Lonny clicked the reins and they started forward.

Millicent ran out onto the porch clutching onto one of the posts.

"Ungrateful girl! I taught you everything you know!" she yelled hoarsely after the departing wagon. Then she slumped against the post and began to sob. No, that wasn't true, she admitted to herself. She hadn't taught Kit *everything* she knew. No one could have taught the girl that kind of loyalty and self-sacrifice.

15

Sitting by Cora's bed, Kit could see out the window. October sunshine spilled over the golden fields, now shorn of their harvest, and the maples along the road, turning red and yellow, edged the meadow with brilliant color. Apple trees in the orchard, heavy with crimson fruit ready to be picked, scented the autumn air with a rich winey scent.

The beauty of the Indian summer day filled Kit with a restless yearning to be out under the cloudless blue sky. Unconsciously she sighed, turning to look at the still figure on the bed.

Cora's face was drawn, cheeks sunken, eyelids closed. Her graying hair in plaits lay on the pillow, the once-busy hands inert on the coverlet.

In all the time Kit had known Cora, she had never seen her like this. All her memories of Cora were of constant movement. Pictures of Cora's thin, nervous figure flickered through Kit's mind — bustling at the stove, wielding a broom, bending over the scrubboard, scattering feed to the chickens in the yard, hoeing in the vegetable garden, stretching, reaching, lifting — always working, always in motion.

Now she lay there hour after hour, day after day, barely moving.

"The whole right side is affected," Dr. Woodward had told them that first night when Kit arrived at the farm with Lonny. "The paralysis may only be temporary. Her speech is impaired, but this, too, may eventually come back. I can't tell how much damage has been done to her brain. We'll just have to wait and see."

Jess's face had looked almost as blank and stiff as Cora's while Dr. Woodward spoke. Kit wasn't even sure he was absorbing what Dr. Woodward was saying. He seemed in a state of shock.

Of course that was understandable. In twenty years Cora had never seemed to have a sick day. She was up and doing within a few days of each of her children's births. Until Kit had come, she had done all the work without any help. Kit felt the seriousness of Cora's illness and the effect it would have on her family had not yet begun to penetrate.

"She'll need to be turned, moved at least three times a day, her limbs gently moved and massaged so the muscles don't atrophy before she gets some flexibility back," Dr. Woodward directed Kit, as if he took for granted that she would be caring for Cora.

That seemed to be what everyone expected. After the first few days, when Cora passed the critical stage and Dr. Woodward said she was out of danger, the Hansen household fell into a routine with Kit managing.

At first, Dr. Woodward had come every day. Then he told Kit that would no longer be necessary. "Now, it is just a matter of time to see if she will recover fully or partially. She may remain like this for a few weeks or a few months or forever." He shook his head. "You simply can't tell with strokes."

Kit had felt her heart sink at this pronouncement.

She had walked with him to the door. Suddenly as if he had just remembered, he turned to her with a frown.

"Weren't you supposed to be off to school, young lady?"

Kit felt herself flinch and she looked away from those kind, concerned eyes.

"Yes, sir, I was, but of course, when Cora was taken sick —" She let her words fade away, speaking for themselves.

"But you had some sort of a scholarship, didn't you?" he persisted.

Kit nodded, feeling the ache in her throat with the effort not to cry at this reminder of what she had given up.

Dr. Woodward stood there for a moment, his face grim, then shook his head and shifted his medical bag from one hand to the other.

"Couldn't Jess have gotten someone else in to help?"

"I don't know. I don't think so. I didn't even think —"

Dr Woodward gave his head another shake.

"What a shame, what a —" He stopped as if wanting to say something stronger. Then he patted Kit's shoulder. "You're a good girl, Kit. A fine, courageous young woman."

Kit saw a mixture of sympathy and admiration in his expression, then he went out the door, down the porch steps, got into his buggy and drove down the road, accompanied by curls of dust.

She stood there watching until his buggy became a small black miniature, moving through the farm gate and along the road back to town. Dr. Woodward's questions had brought back all the longing for freedom, the hope she had known at the prospect of college. For a moment a sharp wave of regret and despair made her weak, and she clutched the porch post for support.

But it lasted only a moment. "Never debate in the darkness a decision made in the light." From somewhere within Kit, those words sprang to mind. They rang in her inner ear as distinctly as a bell. Echoing within her a turning point was reached. She would never look back, she promised herself. The fact was that she had sacrificed her own chance for happiness for a greater, more urgent need. At the time she had made it, she had acted out of a clear call. And she had not wavered in her resolution. Nor would she do so now.

As this realization took hold, Kit felt a conscious sensation that she had moved to a higher realm. From out of the past came the teaching in a long ago Sunday school class: "Obey and the blessing follows."

She had to trust that was true. She would wait patiently for the time of the blessing. It didn't matter if anyone else knew or understood. Kit believed if she "trusted in the Lord, He would bring it to pass."

The woman on the bed moaned slightly and Kit rose quickly, bent over her. Cora's lips were parched, and Kit poured water into a tumbler, then dipped a small folded linen cloth into it and held it to Cora's mouth.

Her heart constricted with pity as she

looked down at her. It was so sad to see her like this. Kit slipped her arm under Cora's bony shoulders and raised her a little so that she could turn the pillow over to its cooler side. Then she smoothed the sheets again.

Only little more than six weeks ago, Cora had been a healthy, vigorous woman. Kit remembered coming out to help cook for the crew Jess had hired during the haying.

Together they had worked from dawn, hauling buckets of water from the well into the house, carrying in armload after armload of firewood for the stove. They had caught chickens, and Kit, her eyes closed, wincing with every stroke, had held them squawking on the block while Cora chopped off the heads. They had scalded and plucked them, then cut them up into pieces and dropped them on the sizzling cast-iron skillet to fry to a crisp golden-brown. Vegetables had to be gathered fresh and boiled or fried, dough mixed for biscuits, cornbread stirred and pans shoved into the oven. All the time the day was heating up, they continued to cook and bake. Desserts were prepared to take the place of the bread baking in the oven — berry cobbler, gingerbread, peach strudel. Men came in from the fields at noon, sweating and hungry, swilling down gallons of lemonade and cold tea. Kit could recall slumping, limp and ragged into kitchen chairs afterwards for a brief rest, themselves too tired to eat, with only this short break until it was time to start over again getting things ready for supper.

A farm wife's work was never done. It was also thankless. Kit found little satisfaction in all the time, energy, and effort that went into food preparation only to be gobbled down by unthinking men whose only goal was filling their stomachs.

That's why she was so grateful to Miss Cady. Miss Cady had shown her a way out of what might have been an inevitable path for Kit, at the Hansens or as a "hired girl" at some other farm. She had awakened a life of the mind and spirit in Kit that could lift her out of this kind of drudgery, open up a whole new world.

Kit felt a twinge of doubt. Would she ever have another chance? Would Miss Cady ever forgive her?

Kit always experienced a heaviness of heart when she thought of Miss Cady. The loss of this cherished relationship pressed down upon her like a physical weight. She had not seen her former teacher since that awful night she had left the cottage under a barrage of recrimination. Kit had not been able to leave Cora, even on Sunday to go into church, where she might have run into her.

Kit sighed heavily, Miss Cady had no understanding of Kit's sense of obligation to Cora, which, in its way was nearly as binding as what she felt for Miss Cady. The two had never liked each other, and Kit had always been caught in the trap of divided loyalty Cora had resented Millicent Cady for all kinds of unnameable reasons, and Miss Cady had deplored Cora's lack of encouragement of Kit's potential. And she actively disliked Jess.

Of course, Miss Cady had been right about Jess. Not by a single word nor gesture had he shown Kit he appreciated her coming. Only a few days after her arrival, she had come down into the kitchen to make some herb tea, hoping to get Cora to sip some much-needed liquid. She had found Jess sitting at his usual place at the table, holding knife and fork in both fists, glowering fiercely.

"When's supper?" he had roared.

Kit had stopped short, the old trepidation of the man's temper gripping her. Then a cold calm overtook her and she faced him unblinkingly.

"I didn't come here to be your hired help,

Jess," she said, purposely using his first name. "I am here to look after Cora. She is my priority and my *only* duty," she said firmly, adding, "I suggest if you and the boys want to eat, you either fix it yourselves, or hire a cook."

With that, she had turned around and busied herself filling the kettle from the kitchen pump. She had not waited to see his reaction. She could only imagine the wrath that must have twisted his expression, the color that might have rushed into his mottled face. In spite of some inner trembling, Kit had gone about her task, and when she left the kitchen to go back upstairs, Jess had gone outside.

Not too much later Kit had heard the rattle of pots and pans and raised voices from the kitchen and assumed the Hansen menfolk were muddling their way through supper.

Not long afterward, Dulcie Meekins had been hired to cook. Kit had won her second battle over her fear of Jess Hansen.

Just then the bedroom door squeaked slightly as it was pushed ajar. Around the corner peered the head and curious face of the tiger-striped tabby, Ginger. She put one cautious foot inside, glanced around warily, then seeing Kit, scooted across the room and made a flying leap into her lap. She curled around twice and settled down, meowing contentedly. Kit rubbed the back of the cat's neck, fondled the satiny ears.

The cat's appearance reminded Kit of the first time she had confronted Jess and the outcome. She smiled, remembering how this cat had come to be so comfortably "at home" in the Hansens' house.

The barn cat had a litter of five kittens and Jess had come in the house one day remarking offhandedly. "Well, that cat's gettin' pretty old. Reckon this'll be the last litter she'll have. I'll keep one out of the bunch and drown the rest."

Kit nearly dropped the dish she was drying.

"Oh, no, you can't!" she had cried in distress.

Jess turned astonished eyes upon her, dumbfounded that she was opposing something he'd said.

Kit had gone down to the barn a couple of times to view the kittens and found them adorable. The thought that anyone would do anything to them as cruel as Jess proposed was unbearable.

"We don't need more'n one cat," he said, glowering at Kit.

Kit glanced over at Cora for help, but

Cora was busy scouring a pot and did not meet her pleading look. Kit screwed up her courage. She was afraid of Jess. She had seen his anger, seen even the agile Caspar and Lonny duck from the back side of his swift hand on more than one occasion, seen them tearfully emerge from the woodshed after an application of his discipline.

But thinking of those dear little furry creatures being tied in a burlap sack weighted with rocks and thrown in the river was too much for Kit's tender heart. Quickly she prayed for inspiration and got it.

"Oh, please, wait! Let me see if I can find homes for them first, before you do anything," she begged. *"Please!"*

To Kit's surprise, Cora broke in. "There ain't no real hurry, is there? Why not let Kit try?"

"We'd have to wait 'til they're weaned if I do that," Jess objected.

"Well, a week or ten days ain't goin' to matter that much, is it?" asked Cora, trying to sound indifferent.

Jess jammed his hands in his overall pockets, made a grunting sound and started back outside mumbling, "Lotta durned foolishness."

"Oh, thank you!" Kit sighed as she let out

a long breath. She might even have hugged Cora except that just then, Cora turned to her, frowning.

"You better do like you said, Kit. I don't fancy buckin' Jess when he's set his mind to do somethin'."

Kit nodded happily. She already knew who she was going to suggest to give the kittens a home.

As it turned out the smallest of the litter died and, of the four that were left, Helene and Toddy each wanted one and Laurel, of course, had to have one, too. That left the fourth, the biggest and strongest, at the Hansens.

Before she had put the three others in a basket to deliver them, Kit named them Wynken, Blynken and Nod from a nursery rhyme she had read to Gwynny at bedtime.

The tawny tiger kitten that was left, she named Ginger, and he became Kit's special pet. Unknown to Jess, she carried him up to her loft bedroom every night where he slept, curled up at the foot of her bed.

Smiling at the memory of the episode years ago, Kit realized that was when she and Cora had become allies. After that, there was an unspoken bond between them that remained to this day.

No matter what, Kit would not forsake

Cora in her time of need. No matter that Jess was still his surly self and did not deserve her sacrifice. No matter that Miss Cady was angry and had irrevocably abandoned Kit. In her heart Kit knew she had done the right thing — the *only* thing.

16

Kit unlocked the door and stepped into the cottage. She took a few tentative steps down the hall and paused for a minute. From where she stood, she could see into the little parlor and on the other side the dining alcove and just beyond that, the tiny kitchen. Suddenly she realized she was holding her breath, and slowly let it out in a long, contented sigh.

Sometimes dreams *do* come true, she thought. Sometimes prayers *are* answered!

Here she was in the cottage where she had dreamed so many dreams, prayed so many prayers. It had been a long time coming, but everything she had ever hoped for was finally happening.

A place of her own, a job, and for the first time a chance to chart her own future.

Setting down her small suitcase, Kit went out into the kitchen. She took some paper from the stack of newspapers by the stove, crumpled it with a few sticks of kindling from the woodbox, opened the stove door and laid a fire. Striking a long match to it, she had a brisk fire going within minutes.

Then, pumping water from the pump near the cast-iron sink, she poured it into the kettle and placed it on the stove. While waiting for the water to boil, Kit looked around her with pleasure.

She moved around slowly, stopping to touch a chair back, smoothing her hand on top of the table, picking up a vase, holding it in her hands for a moment, then putting it down. Everything had happened so fast it was hard to believe.

It had been nearly two years since Cora's stroke, and Kit had gone back to the Hansens to care for her. Her recovery had been slow at first, but little by little Cora had regained the use of her legs; later, she had achieved a halting mobility. Her speech was still garbled but it, too, seemed to be coming back. Dr. Woodward credited this amazing recuperation to Cora's basically strong constitution and to Kit's conscientious nursing. Kit had massaged Cora's limbs, exercised them daily, urged her to push herself, to struggle, not to give in to frustration, to fight to recover her strength and health. This attention had saved Cora from the depression into which so many stroke victims fall by being consistently cheerful and optimistic. Gradually, Kit had helped her to sit up, stand and take those first agonizing steps, holding onto a chair for support and pushing it ahead of her.

Success had been hard-won but, against all odds, Cora was improving.

At the same time, Lonny, the oldest of the Hansen boys, declared he was going to marry Alverna Colby, the daughter of a neighboring farmer. He had been courting Alverna for some time. She was the oldest of eight and capable of taking over at the Hansens without the slightest trouble. Her younger sister would come to give Cora the help she needed in dressing and walking until her recovery was complete.

When Kit realized she was no longer needed and could leave without feeling she was shirking her duty, she felt a sense of unbounded freedom. Almost simultaneously, she heard through Miss Smedley at the library, about the job at the newspaper, the *Meadowridge Monitor* and, armed with references from Mr. Henson and Miss Clemmens, the English teacher, Kit had applied for the position as General Reporter.

The kettle began to whistle, and Kit, knowing just where it was, got down the small, round, brown pottery teapot, found the canister of loose tea, measured it into the pot, then poured in the boiling water, replacing the lid to let it steep. Just the way

Miss Cady had taught her, she thought, smiling ruefully.

This was another stroke of luck, a completely unexpected one. The very same day she got the job, she had seen the FOR RENT, FURNISHED sign on the white picket fence in front of the little shingled cottage where she had lived her last year of high school. Miss Cady's cottage.

Millicent Cady had announced to the School Board that she had accepted another teaching position for the next year and would be leaving Meadowridge at the end of the term in June. Now, in August, the little house was vacant and ready for another tenant.

Waiting for *me!* Kit thought to herself.

Her tea ready, she filled a pink and white china cup, then sat down at the table, staring out into the garden behind the house.

Who would ever have dreamed things would turn out like this? I must write it all down for Jamie and Gwynny was her next thought.

Writing letters to the little lost brother and sister was something Kit had continued to do all these years.

It had become more a private journal for Kit in which she poured all her private

137

thoughts, feelings, the events and happenings of her life. She had almost discarded the childish hope that they would ever read these "letters" or that she would ever find the children. But writing them gave Kit an anchor in a life that seemed to have lost its moorings.

She finished her tea, rinsed out her cup and placed it on the wooden drainboard, then walked through the cottage again. At the end of the hall she hesitated, wondering which bedroom she should use. The larger one had been Miss Cady's, Kit's the smaller one. But the window in that one looked out back where the apple tree was, where birds nested and where in the spring, the wonderful lilac bushes bloomed in a profusion of pale lavender spears. Without another thought, Kit took her belongings into her old room and began unpacking.

One of the first things she did was to take out the picture she had won as a prize in Sunday school long ago, now framed, and hung it over her bed.

Within weeks Kit was settled in the cottage as though it had always been her own, as much as the cubbyhole at the *Monitor* soon became designated as her "office." She walked the few blocks to the paper every morning, got her assignments for that day.

Then, feeling every bit the professional, she went on her rounds, gathering the news items that she would later transfer from her notes into readable material. Afterwards she took it to Mr. Clooney to edit. This process could take a scant twenty minutes, or the piece could remain on his desk for an hour while Kit anxiously awaited his verdict. She would watch him from her vantage point as he read it over. When he laid it aside, it was a signal for her to retrieve it and take the heavily blue-penciled copy back to the composing room for Mac, the printer, to set.

Kit looked forward to each day. She had never felt so alive, so fulfilled, so happy. She loved everything about working at the newspaper. The smell of paper, ink, the sound of the big press on Thursdays when the weekly was "put to bed." When it was printed, she enjoyed opening the fresh new issue, seeing the words she had written in crisp, black print on the crackly white paper.

Granted that, from the beginning, Kit's actual reporting consisted mainly of picking up ad copy from the various Meadowridge stores and businesses and bringing them in for Mr. Clooney to rewrite or lay out for printing. But eventually, with little comment and less direction, he would tell Kit, "Better cover the Town Council meeting tonight," or "Interview Captain Higgins, the Fire Chief, about the possible causes of the barn fire out at the Stratton farm."

As time went on, there were less penciled changes and scratch-throughs on her copy, more grunts and nods as he handed back her copy with a jerk of his thumb, indicating she could deliver it to the back room.

The longer Kit worked at the *Monitor*, the harder it was for her to remember how nervous she had been when applying for the job. Her voice had cracked a little when she asked if the job for a reporter had been illed. Miss Jessica Hadley, who took the classified ads at the high counter at the front, had looked at her with curiously skeptical eyes over her Ben Franklin glasses. Pointing with a pencil she had taken out from behind her ear toward a man with a green eyeshade hunched over a cluttered desk in the corner near the large window that overlooked Main Street she had replied indifferently, "There's Mr. Clooney, the editor. You'll have to see him."

"Never had a woman reporter," Ed Clooney had growled, looking over her letters of recommendation.

Kit had held her breath, hands pressed tightly together, praying that precedent wasn't a prejudice. After all, this was 1902.

Women all over the country were working at jobs once held only by men. Besides, Kit had not seen any other applicants lining up outside the *Monitor* building that morning.

At length, he had handed her back the folder with her credentials, saying, "Well, we can give it a try. When can you start?"

And that is how Kit had been hired.

Those first few weeks had been a combination of trepidation and trials. From the noncommunicative editor, the dubious Miss Hadley, the grouchy printer, the prankish Joe, who was a "jack-of-all-trades" and general flunky, no one at the paper seemed overjoyed or enthusiastic about the new employee. For the most part, Kit might as well have been invisible as she came and went, trying hard to do what she thought was expected of a reporter, but with no real guidelines.

Over the months all of them — Mr. Clooney and Miss Hadley, Mac and Joe — had become her friends; more than friends actually. Kit felt she had learned so much from them, not only about newspapers, but what it meant to work as a team, each contributing a part of a combined, worthwhile effort. Miss Hadley seemed to keep the whole operation going. On the day they went to press, she brought a hamper of food as they worked around the clock to get the weekly edition out. She catered to Mr. Clooney's curmudgeon personality, cajoled Mac, the printer, who was inclined to be testy and temperamental; she both bullied and babied young Joe, the printer's "devil," and reassured and commiserated with Kit on the vagaries of getting a newspaper out and maintaining one's sanity week after week.

By the time Kit had worked at the *Monitor* a year she almost felt she had always been there. That was both comforting and a little frightening. Did she want to become a fixture there like Jessica?

Kit wrote in her letter-journal:

It is fall now in Meadowridge, in some ways the prettiest time of the year here, I think. I love to walk through the fallen leaves along Main Street as I go to work in the morning, hearing them crunch under my feet, breathe in the crisp winey scent of autumn in the air, the woodsmoke mixed with the sweetness of the newly mown hay drifting in from the fields of farms close to town. Even the sunsets, when I'm coming home late in the October afternoons, seem more brilliant somehow.

Sometimes, all this gives me a peaceful feeling inside and, when I come up the path and into this little house, a sense of belonging. But in a deeper sense I feel restless, a kind of melancholy longing that I can't quite define. It's like hearing a train whistle at night as I lie in bed, and wondering where that train is going and whether I should be on it going — where, I don't know — somewhere where I can find what I'm looking for.

The week of Thanksgiving Kit helped put out the *Monitor* a day early so they could take Thursday off. In the morning she attended the service held at the Meadowridge Community Church. She had so much to be thankful for this year, more than any other year of her life. In all the years she had lived with the Hansens, they had never celebrated anything. But the Colby family had always seemed to be a cheerful, good-natured one. So she hoped young Alverna Colby, now Mrs. Lonny Hansen, would bring some of these ways to her new home.

Coming into the church, Kit took a seat at the end of one of the pews. She returned the nods and smiles of people who recognized her. Most everyone knew her now as "that nice young woman from the newspaper."

She was always interested and helpful about getting the Sewing Circle special events in the paper the week before their meeting day, or giving plenty of publicity to the Church Ladies United Christmas Bazaar, as well as spelling all the relatives' names correctly in any write-up of weddings or family reunions on the Social Page. And she could be counted on to write a "lovely obituary" when called upon to do so.

For Kit, it was a good feeling to have found a "place" at last in this town where she had felt an "outsider" for so many years. Then why, more and more, did a vague sense of longing for something else disturb her contentment?

When the organ began playing the opening chords of the first posted hymn, Kit picked up the hymnal and rose with the rest of the congregation to sing, "We gather together to ask the Lord's blessing."

Kit's voice rang out in heartfelt gratitude. The Lord had blessed her with so much, more than she had ever dreamed of, hoped for.

As she sang she became conscious of a sensation of lightness, not only within her, but all around her as though an intense light permeated her body, making her tinglingly aware of everything — the November sunshine slanting through the church windows onto the golden sheaves of wheat along with colorful pumpkins, gourds and Indian corn decoratively arranged in front of the altar rail.

> Come, ye thankful people, come,
> Raise the song of harvest home:
> All is safely gathered in,
> Ere the winter storms begin —

At the close of the hymn, the congregation was seated, settling to hear what their new minister would say. Since the Reverend Brewster's retirement, young Calvin Dinsmore had taken his place in the Meadowridge pulpit. Though the good reverend had recommended him, the Elders had interviewed several other hopefuls, but in the end decided in favor of the man their trusted pastor had suggested. He was still proving himself to the "wait and see" congregation.

"Today is a day we come together with grateful hearts to thank Our Gracious Creator most of all for revealing to us His Son, Jesus Christ. Then we give thanks for His gifts of home, family, friends and bountiful harvest, for the beautiful area in which we live, for minds to think, hearts to love, hands to serve, strength to work, leisure to rest and enjoy. For faithfulness in illness and adversity as well as in prosperity and health.

"On this special day set apart as witness to our gratitude, we acknowledge our dependence on God for all His tender mercies, our thanks for His love, His truth, His forgiveness. Amen."

Seemingly, this brief sermon of a few well-chosen words met with everyone's hearty approval as did his choice of the traditional closing hymn, "Now Thank We All Our God," as at the end of the service, people turned to greet each other with smiles and wishes for the holiday. It was then Kit felt a touch on her shoulder. She turned to see Dan Brooks.

"Dan! What a surprise!" she exclaimed. "What are you doing here?"

He smiled. "I'm spending Thanksgiving with my grandmother and aunts, but, actually I'm on my way to San Francisco."

"San Francisco?"

"Yes, I've been accepted as an intern at a hospital there. I start next week. But it's given me a chance to stop in Meadowridge en route." He paused, looked at her intently. "It's good to see you, Kit. Could we have a cup of coffee somewhere? I'd like to talk. We could go to the coffee shop at Meadowridge

Inn, that is, unless you have plans, have to be somewhere?"

"No. I mean, no plans! I'd love to go," Kit said, a warm feeling of pleasure spreading through her.

They left the churchyard and Dan matched his long stride to Kit's. It was a clear, cold, windless day and the fallen leaves that cluttered the sidewalk crunched underfoot as they started for Front Street and the Meadowridge Inn.

"It's so great to see you, Kit," Dan said, smiling down at her. "I wasn't sure any of the old crowd would be around. I felt sort of like a stranger myself when I walked into church this morning. Then, I saw you and somehow I felt — well, not so much —"

" 'Among the alien corn'?" Kit suggested, laughing.

"Well, I guess you could say something like that, although I never was as good at quotations as you. So, are you still writing, Kit, poetry and that sort of thing."

"Not so much poetry any more, but —" she paused then asked, "You know, don't you, that I work for the *Monitor*? And, of course, that means writing, lots of it, every day."

"I guess that's good discipline for a writer. You do still want to be a writer, don't you, Kit?"

"Dan, I *am* a writer! That's what I *do! And* I get paid for it! Every week." She laughed.

"What I meant was —"

"I know what you meant," Kit assured him. "But I really don't know how to answer your question. My job takes up so much of my time, I don't have much left over for the kind of writing I used to do in high school — essays, poetry."

"You were good, Kit, very good. I remember Miss Cady telling us back in grammar school that you were the only one with *real* talent."

The mention of Miss Cady gave Kit's heart a sad little wrench. The rift between them over her going back to the Hansens instead of using her scholarship had never been bridged. Remembering their last painful scene made Kit search for a quick change of subject.

"Well, tell me about *you,* Dan. I think it's very exciting about you going to San Francisco, California. Is it a big hospital?"

"Yes, but the important thing is that it's connected with the University Medical School where they're doing some great research, testing new kinds of treatments."

By this time they had reached the Inn and Dan put his hand on Kit's elbow as they mounted the steps. The Meadowridge Inn had once been a stagecoach stop and had been restored with several new additions over the last several years. The exterior of the rambling clapboard building had a certain rustic charm, but inside it had been refurbished to resemble a fine, modern hotel.

Off the lobby was the restaurant annex where breakfast and lunch were served in a more informal atmosphere than the adjoining elegant dining room provided. They were shown to a table in a sunny corner where they could see out to the town park. A waitress in a crisp blue uniform and ruffled apron brought them coffee and rolls. When she left they both started talking at once.

"I guess you knew —"

"I just heard —"

They stopped, started again. Then, laughing, Dan said, "You first, Kit. You probably know a great deal of what I was going to ask you anyway." He circled his coffee mug with both hands. "Of course, I *do* know Laurel is in Boston. I went by to see Dr. Woodward when I got into town day before yesterday, but he didn't seem to know or at least he did not have much to say about what she was doing or —" he sighed — "when or even *if* she was coming back."

Kit felt that old familiar twinge of yearning as she saw Dan's jaw tighten. He's still in love with Laurel, she thought. Sympathy overrode her own longing. She knew too well how unreturned love felt. Impulsively, she reached over and patted Dan's hand.

"You know, Dan, Laurel always had this need, this obsession, really, to go back to Massachusetts, to Boston, to trace her real family. She talked about it many times when we were alone together. Until that is satisfied, I don't believe Laurel is ready for anything else."

"But, in every way that counts the Woodwards *are* her family," protested Dan, although he spoke without conviction.

Kit nodded. "I know, but she said to me once, 'Nothing ever makes up for being an orphan.'"

"But, *you* — and Toddy, too —" Dan began.

"Both our situations were different." Kit gave a wry little smile. "*Very* different."

"What about Toddy?" he asked. "I went by the Hale house and it was all closed up. There was even a padlock on the front gate. Not a sign of life anywhere."

"Mrs. Hale took them to Europe. They're traveling. I think they've gone to several health resorts. Mrs. Hale keeps hoping to find something, someone who can help poor Helene."

"So, what does that mean for Chris?

For Toddy and Chris?"

Slowly Kit shook her head. "I don't know. I'm not sure. I heard Chris left the University his second year, went to South America on a construction job."

The waitress came by with a steaming coffeepot and refilled their mugs. Dan stirred sugar into his coffee thoughtfully.

"Things have sure changed."

"Are you surprised? You've been away three years, Dan. Didn't you expect them to change?"

He looked up, startling her with the intensity of his brown gaze.

Imperceptibly Kit drew in her breath. She thought she had outgrown her feelings for Dan, thought she had blotted them out of her memory. It was too painful to carry her secret yearning, too complicated, too costly to risk the growing barrier between herself and her dear friend Laurel. She thought, also, that she had almost forgotten what he looked like, but she was surprised by the familiarity of his features — the strong chin and sensitive mouth — and alarmingly disturbed when she looked into those searching eyes.

"*You* haven't changed, Kit," he said, then frowned. "Have you?"

"Nothing ever stays the same, Dan," she

151

replied quietly, while her heartbeat quickened, keeping pace with a rising current of excitement.

"I guess you're right." Dan sighed. "Maybe, when you've been away as long as I have — new situations, new people, new challenges — you like the thought that all the things and people left behind — your hometown, the people you grew up with, cared about, loved — are the same, the one constant. Kind of a safety valve. Know what I mean?" Then he shook his head again. "I guess you don't. You didn't leave."

"That doesn't mean that I won't someday. Don't think I plan to stay at the *Monitor* forever," Kit retorted, the color coming into her cheeks.

Dan was startled by the quick reply. He looked at Kit again, scrutinized her face — her complexion now tinged with pink, the smooth high brow, the clear, intelligent eyes. Those eyes! Why hadn't he noticed them before? They were lovely — sort of a silvery-gray and fringed with the most extraordinary dark lashes.

"You know you ought to, Kit," he said slowly, "think seriously about it, I mean. There's a whole big world out there. Lots of newspapers. You could get a job anywhere writing, reporting. Travel around the world, probably, if you wanted to."

"I intend to!" said Kit, feeling a new kind of excitement rise up within her. Until now, she had not had a chance to talk to anyone about her dreams, her ambitions, and as they spilled out to Dan, she realized they had been there all along, needing only a friendly word of encouragement to stir them to life.

They talked on, oblivious to the time, until Kit suddenly noticed the waiters in the dining room, setting up for the midday dinner service. Many Meadowridge families celebrated Thanksgiving by eating out at the Inn and it was nearly noon.

"We'd better be going."

"Yes, I guess so," Dan agreed reluctantly, "I think Grandmother and the aunties plan to serve dinner at one."

Outside on the porch of the Inn, Dan issued an unexpected invitation. "What about you, Kit? Will you come home with me and have Thanksgiving dinner with us?"

"Thank you, Dan, but no. Miss Hadley, at the paper, is cooking dinner for all of the staff —" She paused, laughing a little. "All of us 'orphans' are spending the holiday together. She's alone, and Mr. Clooney's been a widower for years, and I don't know if Mac's ever been married, but I know he lives by himself, and Joe — well, it will be nice for us all." She smiled.

Again Dan thought how radiant Kit looked when she smiled. She was no beauty like Laurel, but this girl had a shining quality about her.

"Well then, I guess this is goodbye, Kit. I'm due out on the early train tomorrow. It's been wonderful seeing you, having a chance to talk. I'm so glad we had this time together."

"I am too, Dan. And I wish you every success. I know you'll make a fine doctor."

They stood there for a minute, not saying anything, each unwilling to make the first move.

"I have to stop by the cottage," Kit said at last, "pick up a salad I made, my contribution to Miss Hadley's dinner, although I'm sure she won't need it. She usually cooks enough for a small army." She hesitated a second longer. "I'd better be on my way."

"Goodbye, Kit."

"Goodbye, Dan. God bless!" she said, then turning up her coat collar, she hurried away.

At the corner, she turned for one last look. Dan was still standing where she had left him. Smiling, she lifted her hand and waved.

17

Kit stood next to the editor's desk, antici-pating his reaction to her decision. He had turned away from his cluttered oak roll-top and stared silently out onto the town square. Past Mr. Clooney's hunched shoulder, Kit could see out to the dreary winter day. Rain slanted in silvery-blue streaks and streamed down the windowpane.

Finally he swivelled around toward her, the ancient chair squeaking in protest, and scowled at her over his glasses.

"Well, miss, if you've made up your mind to go, I can't stop you," he grunted. "You're not going to find it easy on a big city news-paper, let me tell you that. You're a fine re-porter, Kit, I've no complaints. You can cover anything and cover it well. But some editors and reporters still don't accept the idea of 'lady newspaper writers' except for the Society pages or cooking hints!"

He held up his hand, staving off the argu-ment that sprang immediately to her lips. "I know, I know what you're going to say. It's the twentieth century! Just tell that to the managing editor of some city newspaper! If they hire you at all —"

"They *have* hired me, Mr. Clooney!" Kit interrupted, thrusting forward her letter of confirmation received in the morning's mail.

Ignoring it, he went on, "Be that as it may — I still say, *if* they hire you at all, they'll have you out on the worst assignments — interviewing a fireman who had to climb a tree to rescue some old lady's cat, or worse than that, the mother of an ax murderer who claims her son was 'always a good boy'! They'll run you ragged and pay you less than the men, and hope they'll discourage and wear you out enough so you'll quit."

"*You* did that, Mr. Clooney, and it didn't discourage me."

"I did no such thing!" he denied indignantly. "I had you cover what was going on in Meadowridge that day! If that happened to be some scared cat or interviewing some lady who won First Prize for quilting at the County Fair, that was what we assigned you."

Kit didn't argue, just stood there watching Mr. Clooney squirm uncomfortably, rearranging the piles of scattered notes on his desk. At length, he growled. "I suppose you want a recommendation from me?"

"Yes sir, I'd appreciate that."

"Well, I'll think about it. I mean, that's asking a lot, I'd say. Give you a good send-off to another newspaper when I'm losing the best reporter I've ever had."

Kit smiled and said gently, "Thank you, Mr. Clooney."

Turning away to go back to her own desk, Kit paused. "I do want you to know how much this job has meant to me, sir. I've learned so much from you and —"

He waved her away impatiently. "Go on, go on, don't try to sweet-talk your way out of leaving me in a lurch like this! Who am I going to get to replace you? Who that can at least spell and write a readable sentence?"

"I've talked to Mr. Henson at the High School, Mr. Clooney. He has several bright students, all Seniors, who would jump at a chance to work here."

Mr. Clooney pushed his green eyeshade back from his brow.

"You talking about some kid, not dry behind the ears yet? Working here?" he barked. "You trying to push me into an early grave? I got better things to do with my time in this office than conducting spelling bees for kids and correcting compositions!"

Kit hid her amusement at Mr. Clooney's raving. In the more than two years she had worked at the *Monitor*, she had learned that his proverbial bark was worse than his bite. When the pupil was sincere and willing to learn, Ed Clooney was an inspired teacher. The *Monitor* was his life and he took pride in its clean copy and well-written articles. If he had to, he would tirelessly train somebody he thought had the makings of a good news-paperman. Kit had come to respect him, and regarded his prickly temperament with affectionate tolerance. Her training here had provided her with enough confidence to apply to five California newspapers, and get an acceptance from one.

For the next several weeks Kit worked hard to help smooth the transition after her leaving. Mr. Clooney had reluctantly agreed to give two of the Seniors a trial run, and Kit took on the job of tutoring them, initiating them into the routine of newspaper writing. She oversaw their efforts, suggesting changes, correcting copy and encouraging them. The results were much better than Mr. Clooney had expected and, until he could find a full-time reporter, he had agreed to use the two students.

The last two weeks before Kit left for San

Francisco were busy ones. There was so much to do to get ready for the long trip, the new life into which she was heading. There were also some old doors to close before she could open the many new ones before her.

One thing she had yet to do was to make a trip out to the Hansen farm to tell Cora goodbye.

One cold February afternoon she borrowed Mr. Clooney's mare, Tilly, and his ramshackle buggy and set out for the farm.

As she rattled over the familiar road, now rutted by winter storms, many memories flooded over Kit. Some were hurtful ones that Kit did not allow herself to explore. She had tried to deal with the pain she had encountered as learning experiences, and she was determined not to let them embitter her.

When she reached the farm, Kit led the horse under the shelter of a lean-to next to the barn. She got a worn horse blanket from under the buggy seat and settled it over Tilly's back to keep the chill off the old mare while she was inside. Then she slipped a feeding bucket of oats over her nose.

After that she hurried through the gray drizzle up to the house. Kit's knock was answered by Cora's daughter-in-law, Alverna. On her hip was a rosy-cheeked baby who looked remarkably like Lonny.

"Oh, come in, Kit," she said. "Cora will be so pleased to see you."

Kit stepped into the warmth of the kitchen and sniffed appreciatively. Something gingery was baking. Starched curtains at the windows and a bright cross-stitched cloth on the table gave the room a cheerful air on this dark winter day. Kit noticed an arrangement of dried statice and straw flowers in a dark blue glass holder on the pine hutch.

"Everything looks so nice, Alverna," she commented, looking around.

"Well, thank you, Kit. You know Lonny's Ma likes things to look nice, so I try to please her."

As Kit followed Alverna up the narrow steps leading to the second floor and to the bedroom Cora now occupied, she remembered her own first attempts at bringing bits of beauty into this stark farmhouse years ago. She recalled how very slow Cora had been to appreciate her efforts and support them.

At the top of the stairs, Alverna knocked at one of the doors, then opened it and leaned in.

"Ma, you've got company. Here's Kit to see you."

Kit entered the room as the woman sitting in the rocker by the window slowly turned her head. Every time she came to see Cora, Kit was shocked to see her gradual decline. After a time of improvement, she had taken a turn for the worse. She was thin now to the point of gauntness. Her hair was nearly white and her eyes sunken into deep sockets in her deeply lined face. The effects of her paralysis still showed in her twisted smile, leaving one side of her face unmoved. Her speech was garbled, and it was necessary to listen very closely to understand her words.

Kit pulled a straight chair over close to Cora and sat down. Taking one gnarled hand in both of hers, she looked into the woman's dull eyes.

"I'm going away, Cora. I have a job with a newspaper in San Francisco, California. So I'm leaving Meadowridge next week."

There was little change in Cora's expression, but she nodded her head so Kit knew she had heard and understood. Kit always tried to make her visits as cheerful as possible, knowing how narrow and limited Cora's existence must be. Since her stroke, she was no longer able to do the work that kept her life busy and full. Kit kept up a lively account of Meadowridge news that might interest Cora, about the town, church and other community events.

After about fifteen minutes, just when Kit was running out of things to say, Alverna reappeared with a tray on which was a pot of tea and a plate of freshly baked gingersnaps.

"Thought you ladies would like a little refreshment," she said, setting the tray on the dresser. She handed Kit a cup and saucer, offered her a cookie then proceeded to place a clean napkin on Cora's lap and pour a small portion of tea into a cup and hold it for Cora to sip. Seeing Alverna's tenderness with her mother-in-law touched Kit and ended any lingering guilt she had felt about leaving the farm and the care of Cora to others.

Cora mumbled something that sounded unintelligible to Kit, but evidently Alverna understood.

"Yes, Ma, I'll show her." And she gave Kit a knowing look. "Wait until you see."

The younger woman went over to a shelf and brought back a thick scrapbook, which she laid on Kit's lap. "Open it," she instructed.

To Kit's amazement, inside on page after page were pasted articles she had written for the *Monitor*, ones printed after Mr. Clooney decided to give her a byline for special features.

Kit felt a lump form in her throat, and she looked over at Cora who seemed to be trying to smile.

"I think Ma's tired, Kit," Alverna whispered as she took the scrapbook away and replaced it on the shelf.

Cora had visibly slumped in her chair, and Kit got to her feet at once. She leaned over and kissed Cora's cheek.

"I have to leave now, Cora. Take care of yourself and I'll see you when I come back to Meadowridge."

Their eyes met, and a kind of communication passed between them, deeper than any words. Cora made a sound, and Kit leaned closer to make it out. Not understanding, she simply nodded and patted Cora's shoulder, feeling the boniness under the calico dress.

At the bedroom door, she turned and looked back and thought she saw a tear trickle slowly down the wrinkled face.

"Ma's kept everything you've written, Kit," Alverna said, on the way downstairs. "Even though she don't read, she recognized your name, Kathleen Ternan."

Riding back into town, Kit began to cry. The tears gathered in her eyes and flowed unchecked.

It seemed implausible that she should be tearful on this eve of her new adventure. She had made the choice. The goal she had set for herself was about to be accomplished; the future, bright. Her life's journey had begun. What lay ahead of her promised all sorts of rewards.

So why was she feeling both sadness and some regret for what she was leaving behind? Could she have done more for Cora? She wasn't sure. All she knew, all she prayed was that, somehow, she had made a difference in her life, after all.

18

San Francisco

Kit had always imagined California as a land of perpetual sunshine, of orange groves and tropical palms. It was rather a shock to discover that San Francisco could be cool with a brisk, ocean-blown breeze, misty mornings, and early evenings of swirling fog.

This was not entirely a disappointment. The fog lent a mysterious aura to a city she found constantly surprising and interesting. Since Kit had always loved the romantic English novels of the wind-tossed moors and fog-bound seaports, San Francisco fascinated her.

Kit arrived in the city on an overcast day with hovering gray clouds, and a sharp, salty wind blowing off the Bay. Upon her arrival she went directly to the newspaper, clutching the letter she had received with confirmation of her employment as a reporter just in case something had happened in the interim and they had forgotten about her.

After a suspenseful, doubt-ridden wait, her hiring was confirmed and she was told to start work the following Monday. She was then handed some forms to fill out. When she ventured the fact she did not as yet have an address to put in the appropriate line, she was sent down to Classified. There a helpful clerk gave Kit a list of room rentals within reasonable distance from the newspaper building.

Armed with these and rather dazed by all the new things that were happening to her all at once, Kit set out. Her uncharted future here in this busy metropolis, unpredictable as it seemed, caused some inner apprehension as well as a certain excitement.

She had to stop and ask directions several times to find the various addresses given. As she climbed steep hills and trudged up countless steps to inquire about rooms advertised, she was often told that the place was already rented, or that the only available room was a double and she would have to share it, or when she reached it, saw a NO VACANCY sign in the window. Her suitcase was getting heavier and heavier each time she had to pick it up and carry it to the next possibility. With only three more addresses on her list, Kit began to get discouraged.

Near the end of the day, she rang the bell of a hillside house, and the door was opened by a sallow-faced woman, with a suspicious glint in her eyes. She told Kit she had a room, but warned her before she showed it that she always required a month's rent in advance.

Weary, but determined not to be intimidated, Kit followed her up a long staircase to the second floor. She prayed the room would be decent, clean and acceptable. She was beginning to experience some gnawing anxiety about the big step she had taken, leaving Meadowridge, coming so far from the only home she had ever really known.

At the top of the stairs, the woman opened the door and led the way in.

"Most people like a front room and this one rents for six dollars a week — *payable in advance.* I rent these rooms by the month because I don't like people comin' and goin'. I like my renters permanent. You get a better class of roomers when you insist on that," she declared. "If they leave before the month's up, don't matter for what reason, I don't give a refund. That's my policy. I always tell people beforehand so there's no misunderstanding."

Kit nodded and walked to the center of the

room, looking around. There was a brass bed, a washstand with a pitcher and bowl, a bureau with a mirror, a table by the bay window, two straight chairs.

"The bathroom's down the hall . . . you sign up for baths. The nights or days for this room, Number Four, is Tuesdays and Fridays." The woman leaned against the door frame, arms folded, waiting for Kit's decision.

Suddenly Kit felt exhausted. The long train trip from Meadowridge, with two hectic changes in St. Louis and Chicago, the uncertainty of the new life she was starting, the tiring day-long trek looking for a place to live had all begun to weigh upon her. She was anxious to get settled.

"I'll take it," she said, opening her purse to take out the month's rent.

The woman counted out the bills Kit handed her.

"Well, that's that then," she said when she was satisfied that the money was all there. "I'll give you a receipt when I bring up your clean sheets and towels. By the way, I'm Mrs. Bredesen." And she went out the door, closing it behind her.

Going to the window, Kit drew aside the stiff net curtains and looked down into the busy street below. Judging from the purposeful stride of the pedestrians, everyone seemed to have someplace important to go. Kit felt at once thrilled and threatened. Soon she would be among them, starting her new work, carrying out assignments, getting acquainted. For, of all the people in this vast city, she didn't know a single solitary soul — except for Dan Brooks.

A brisk knock on the door interrupted her thoughts and Mrs. Bredesen reappeared with an armload of sheets and towels.

"You get clean linens once a week, towels twice. There's a laundry chute at the end of the hall. You put your used ones down it on Fridays."

"Thank you," murmured Kit, taking the pile from her.

Then Mrs. Bredesen pointed to a card pasted to the inside of the door. "These here are my rules for roomers. There's to be no cooking of any kind in the rooms. No entertaining or guests of the opposite sex above the first floor. You may receive visitors in the downstairs parlor. The front door is locked at 11 P.M. sharp. I don't open it after that unless for a real emergency. I keep a decent house. I'm a tee-totaler myself, and if my roomers do otherwise that's their business, unless it interferes with mine," she said emphatically. "I keep a decent house and I expect my roomers to obey the rules."

Kit, who wasn't expecting any visitors and certainly had not planned to entertain, listened, nodding solemnly until Mrs. Bredesen finished.

"Well, I guess that's all," the woman concluded. "You won't be taking any meals here, I guess? That's extra, of course. Some of my roomers do. They find it more convenient and more economical than getting it downtown. I serve one meal a day, dinner at six o'clock on the dot. For fifty cents a week extra I put out coffee and rolls in my dining room in the morning. If you want that, you have to sign up."

"I'll let you know, thank you," Kit said quietly, wishing the landlady would leave. She was almost dizzy from fatigue and longed to be alone so she could settle her thoughts and unpack.

Finally the woman was gone and Kit locked the door. She took off her shoes, wiggling her toes, and walked from one small cotton scatter rug to the other over to the bed and sat down. After nearly a week of travel, she felt an enormous sensation of relief to be at last somewhere she could call her own. At least, for a month.

That thought reminded her of the amount

just subtracted from her small cash reserve. When she had withdrawn her savings from the Meadowridge Bank, she had felt rich. But, Kit had discovered traveling was costly despite her efforts to be frugal. Besides her one-way ticket to California there had been unexpected expenses en route. She had been delayed twice, with missed connections and late arriving trains and had no alternative than to spend money on food.

Kit emptied the contents of her purse on the bed to count what was left of what had seemed an adequate little nestegg upon her departure from Meadowridge. She felt a small twinge of alarm but refused to allow it to surface. She would be careful, and in two weeks she would collect her first paycheck. Then things would work out.

"Everything works together for good for those who love the Lord and are called to His purpose," Kit reminded herself.

She was putting things back into her purse when she came upon a small square of pink paper. She unfolded it and saw it was Dan's address. Studying it, she remembered the incident with his mother.

One of the last days she had been in Meadowridge, Kit was doing some last-minute shopping. Standing at the counter in the dry goods store, someone had touched her arm.

"Kit? Kathleen Ternan?" the woman at her elbow asked.

Kit had not recognized her until she introduced herself.

"I'm Vada Brooks," she said. "Daniel Brooks's mother."

"Oh, yes! I'm sorry I —"

"Of course I didn't expect you to know me. We only met that once, at Graduation. You were naturally too excited and happy to remember me. But then you made a great impression on me. On everyone, I should think. Dan always spoke so highly of you." She paused, fidgeting a little nervously as if she wasn't sure what she was going to say next. "And of *all* his friends here, of course. You know he's doing his residency now in a San Francisco hospital?"

Kit had the grace to blush.

"Yes, I know," she replied. "I saw Dan when he was here last Thanksgiving."

"He's doing very well," Mrs. Brooks said in her quick, anxious way, then added, "but he's very lonely. Not that he doesn't have friends among the other young doctors there, the hospital staff. Dan makes friends easily. He is so likable —" her voice trailed off vaguely. "I heard, Miss Ternan, that *you* were leaving Meadowridge your-self, going to work on a newspaper in Cal-ifornia, a San Francisco paper."

Kit nodded, wondering what in the world the woman had on her mind.

"Miss Ternan, I was thinking . . . seeing you and Dan were in the same class, grew up here together . . . that is, rather *when,* you get to San Francisco . . . would you let Dan know? I'm sure he would so enjoy seeing somebody from home — an old friend. May I give you his address?" Mrs. Brooks asked, already fumbling in her handbag for a piece of notepaper and a pencil.

Now, as she held the small slip of paper in her hand, Kit read it over. Was that one of those chance encounters, or was there something significant about her running into Dan's mother that day just before she left?

To be truthful, why else had she chosen to apply to newspapers in northern California except on the slim chance that somehow she might see Dan? Kit asked herself. She re-placed the note with the scribbled address in the compartment of her handbag, then leaned back against the bed pillows wearily. Slowly her eyes closed and before she knew it she had drifted off into an exhausted sleep.

★ ★ ★

The next thing she was aware of was the gray light of dawn illuminating the unfamiliar room. Outside, she could hear the sound of wagon wheels on the street below. The city was coming awake, going about its business of the day. And she was part of it, Kit thought, coming slowly awake. She was actually in San Francisco, about to start her career as a journalist.

19

Even though Kit no longer believed that the letters she wrote to Jamie and Gwynny would ever be read by either of them, out of long habit she started her journal entry as she always had:

Dear Jamie and Gwynny,
    San Francisco is a big, exciting city. Never in my wildest dreams did I ever imagine anything like it nor did I ever expect to live here.
    The city was built on hills, so you will not be surprised to learn that I live in a house on top of a hill. If I lean way out over my windowsill, I can see the Bay and Ferry Building, where the boats come, bringing people from Sausalito, Martinez, Berkeley, and Oakland. From early in the morning, this lower part of Market Street is alive with all sorts of activity — crowds of people, horse-drawn streetcars with clanging bells, carriages and cabs. But the most amazing kind of transportation are the red cable cars.

From a distance they look like toys, running up and down the steep hills on rails, pulled by a steel cable which moves in a slot underneath the surface of the street. The first time I rode on one, I was terrified! But you, Jamie, would love them! You always did like scary things — scary stories, being pushed higher and higher on the swings in the park —

Downtown, where I go every morning to my job at the newspaper office, the sidewalks are packed with people, all hurrying somewhere. There is such a variety of them. I love to see the Chinese with their slanted eyes and pale skin, in blue cotton coats and trousers, carrying baskets of vegetables on poles. In contrast are the well-dressed businessmen, in black frock coats, brocaded vests, and gold watch chains. Then there are the miners down from their mines in the Sierra Hills. Usually they have stubby beards, broad-brimmed felt hats, somewhat the worse for wear, flannel shirts and boots. But for all their scraggly appearance, they are some of the richest men in California.

The city, too, has its many faces. On Montgomery Street, the scene changes. Here are expensive shops with all sorts of beautiful things for sale — dress salons and jewelry stores, millinery shops with hats displayed in their windows that must rival those to be found in Paris, fabric stores displaying yards of gorgeous materials — satins, embroidered silks, rich velvets. Here you see the most elegantly dressed people promenading — young men with gold-and-ivory-headed canes and polished hats, escorting ladies in stylish outfits and handsome jewelry.

The buildings here are all several stories high and of every style of architecture, each one seemingly trying to outdo the next in magnificence, size, and splendor. There are mansions like palaces, built by millionaires, in a fashionable section called Nob Hill that are said to be even more incredible inside — marble statues, huge oil paintings, gilded furniture, and treasures gathered from all sorts of exotic places.

There is a contagious undercurrent of excitement here that you can actually feel as you walk along the streets, as if everyone is on the brink of something new, intriguing, or spectacular. One has the sense of expectation, as if anything were possible, that all one's dreams could come true. And why not? You are sur-rounded by dozens of such examples!

My job, of course, has none of the glamour, the color, the excitement of the city. I don't know really if I expected it to be otherwise. After all, I am lucky to have been taken on with only a small-town weekly newspaper experience. Besides that, I fear, even in 1905, there is a preju-dice against the "working woman." My immediate boss, Clem Stoniger, is an "old-timer," a veteran reporter with a wealth of newspaper and life experience behind him. He has had what they call a "checkered career." In his youth he stowed away on a ship and sailed all over the world. Coming around Cape Horn, he landed in California as a kid of six-teen, just about the time the Gold Rush broke. He went with all the others in search of wealth and fortune and he worked a couple of claims, but finally his health broke. Instead of finding gold, he ended up writing about it for eastern newspapers before settling here in San Francisco as a reporter.

He has helped me a great deal. Though most of my duties are dull and routine — checking tax lists, accident re-ports (these caused mainly by an excess number of vehicles, plus reckless drivers), and obituaries — Mr. Stoniger tells me to be patient. "Your time will come," he tells me. "Sometimes it's just being in the right place at the right time. You never know when you'll get your chance to report the *big* story."

I hope he's right. In the meantime, I try to record my impressions, descriptions of people, incidents I observe. It is all part of becoming a writer, which is what I really want to be —

Dear Jamie and Gwynny,

I have been in San Francisco for three months now, and have grown to love it. This little room seems as if I've always lived here. I've hung the "Guardian Angel" picture — the one I won in Sunday school years ago — over my bed. The afghan Cora gave me is folded at the end.

Each day brings something new. Mr. Stoniger has been giving me small writing assignments, and he hands them back to me heavily blue-penciled with questions like: WHO? WHAT? WHEN? WHERE? WHY? scribbled in the margins. He is teaching me the basics of good reporting. "This isn't Meadowridge or

Podunk, Kit. *This* is San Francisco, *this* is the big time. This isn't a country journal, this is a city newspaper," he'll growl at me. At first, I was not only in awe of him, I was afraid of him. But now I realize he is only trying to help me write more accurately.

"You've the makings of a feature writer, Kit," he told me one day when he returned from a longer than usual lunch hour, mellowed, I'm sure, with the help of accompanying liquid refreshment. "Rewrite — that's what makes the difference. Check your facts, then write from the heart."

On my days off, I like to walk. San Francisco is conducive to wandering, I walk down to the Wharf and watch the fishing boats come in and the fishermen unload their catch. There is a kind of beautiful rhythm to their movements. As they work, they call to each other, speaking in Italian, a language with a lilting quality. The fishermen seem a good-natured bunch, evidently loving their jobs, which is, I suppose, the real secret of happiness. To love what you're doing. I certainly do!

I turned a piece in to Mr. Stoniger the other day, a "human interest" story about a miner who had made and lost several fortunes in the gold field, and was going back up to find the "Lost Dutchman" mine. He swore he knew exactly where it was. He was seventy if he was a day, but he still has "gold fever" and was convinced *this* time he was going to overcome all the pitfalls of the past. Mr. Stoniger read it, grunted, and handed it back to me, saying, "You're getting there, Kit, you're getting there," which is about the nicest compliment he's yet paid me.

I've been writing Mr. Clooney and the others at the *Meadowridge Monitor* since I've been here, telling them about San Francisco, describing the sights and scenes. Jessica wrote me that Mr. Clooney wants me to do a regular feature for them. Not only will I be paid for it, but I'll have my own byline — "City Sights and Insights" by Kathleen Ternan.

Dear Jamie and Gwynny,

Guess what? Dan Brooks showed up at the newspaper yesterday, asking for me! One of his aunts had cut out my column in the *Meadowridge Monitor* and sent it to him, so he decided to look me up! My heart nearly stopped when I saw him standing there. He's filled out, and even though he seems taller, he's still the best-looking fellow in our entire graduating class, at least in my opinion. He wanted to make plans for his next day off from the hospital. When I told him the day I would be free, he said he was sure he could switch with one of the other residents.

We didn't have time to exchange much Meadowridge news. I guess we will next Thursday. I started to ask him about Laurel, but something stopped me. Why am I so happy? I shouldn't start to dream about him again. We're just good friends, both alone and lonely in the big city. He was glad to see a familiar face, that's all. Don't get any ideas, Kit Ternan!

Dear Jamie and Gwynny,

It is nearly midnight and I should be in bed since my alarm goes off at six, but I'm too excited to sleep. I have had the most marvelous day, and I want to put it all down before I forget any of it, not that I think I ever shall!

I was ready and waiting when Dan came by to get me about ten o'clock this morning. I was so happy to see him. We both mentioned how strange it is that we ended up in San Francisco, so far from Meadowridge. Maybe more so for me. It's different now that I'm on my own. Dan seems to think it's quite remarkable that I have a job on a big city newspaper and that I seem to know my way around the city. I told him it was all trial and error, that I'd gotten lost plenty of times when learning my way around!

It was a glorious day, the kind San Franciscans like to brag about. Sunny and clear, cloudless skies, a sharp wind off the Bay, making little dancing whitecaps all across the dark blue water. We walked all over, a hundred miles, it seemed! Dan wanted to see everything, go everywhere, said he'd been so cooped up in the hospital on the merciless residents' schedule that he felt as if he'd been let out of prison.

"You haven't changed your mind about wanting to be a doctor, have you?" I asked, a little worried.

"Oh, no, I'm looking forward to being a country doctor. Did I tell you Dr. Woodward has practically promised me that when I finish, I can come and work with him?" Dan asked me.

I felt my heart sink. That meant Dan would be leaving San Francisco at the end of his residency.

"No, you never told me. But, of course, this is the first time we've seen each other since last November."

"That's right," Dan said as we walked on a little further. "I've thought a lot about that Thanksgiving Day, Kit."

I was curious to know *what* he had thought, but that was all he said just then. We were walking up one of these hills that absolutely takes all your breath, so neither of us said much until later.

We walked along the bluffs above the beach. Dan couldn't get enough of the ocean — watching the surf, looking way out to where the big ships glide along the horizon, carrying cargo to ports everywhere in the world. Even where we were, we could feel the salt spray. The wind was blowing so hard, it practically tore the hairpins out of my hair, tossing it into tangles.

Then we went to Chinatown with all its queer little stores, and Dan decided he wanted to try some real Chinese food. He even insisted on eating with chopsticks! I tried, but finally asked the waiter for a fork before I starved to death! Dan struggled stubbornly and managed pretty well.

Afterwards, we wandered in and out of the shops. There were beautiful teakwood screens for sale, boxes, trunks, carved ivory and jade, not just the green kind, but pale pink and lavender, too, jewelry and delicate figurines. Some of the shops are very expensive, others just junk. We had a good time, pretending we had all the money in the world and buying gifts for everyone we knew.

In the late afternoon, we walked down to Fisherman's Wharf. By now it was getting colder, so we stopped at a little café for "espresso," a kind of steamed coffee with a dollop of whipped cream on top. This warmed us up right away. Since Dan didn't have to report back to the hospital until eleven P.M., he insisted on taking me to dinner.

When I hesitated, fearing he didn't know the kind of prices charged at San Francisco restaurants, he seemed to have read my mind. "Don't worry!" he said. "This is on Uncle Ned. He sent me a fifty in his letter today, told me to find a pretty girl and take her out 'on the town.' Those were his exact words! So I've found the pretty girl. Now where shall we go for dinner?"

I didn't say any more, just begged him

to let me come by my room and freshen up a bit so we could go out to dine in a style befitting the occasion.

On the way, Dan talked about how good and generous his uncle had been to him all through his college years, med school, and the lean years of interning and residency.

"If it hadn't been for Uncle Ned, I'd never have made it," Dan told me confidentially. Of course Dan himself has done all the usual things to help make ends meet — stoking furnaces, waiting on tables, and mowing lawns. Still it was hardly enough to give him much *extra* money.

"Uncle Ned always seemed to know when I needed it most, and he always came through," Dan said gratefully.

Dan, speaking of his uncle, triggered the memory of an incident when Miss Cady had been disdainful of Ned Morris. I remember particularly one spring evening when Miss Cady and I were walking over to the high school for a combined recital given by the Music and Drama Club and Dan and his uncle had come along in Mr. Morris's open buggy. He stopped immediately and offered us a ride, and Miss Cady had coolly turned him down. After they'd driven off, I'd asked her why she had refused. She seemed indignant that I didn't know.

"We shouldn't be seen in public with a man who runs a pool hall, Kit!"

"Mr. Morris seems as nice as he can be," I said mildly.

"He's no gentleman, or he'd find another line of work!" she snapped.

"Dan told me his uncle is going to put him through college and medical school." I couldn't resist sharing this information since she was being so snobbish. "Dan says he couldn't possibly go if Mr. Morris wasn't paying the fees."

"That has nothing to do with the proper thing for us to do, Kit," Miss Cady said, annoyed with me for questioning her action.

I almost reminded her how she had always taught that any kind of work was noble unless it was dishonest. But she seemed so offended by this exchange already that I bit my tongue and decided to let the subject drop. I think it was that incident that made me realize, perhaps for the first time, that Miss Cady was not always right. Just because you admire someone doesn't mean you can't disagree with them.

Anyway, the reason I write this down at all is that, just as I was thinking about Miss Cady, Dan suddenly said, "You know, Uncle Ned was always in love with Millicent Cady. Of course, he knew it was hopeless since she didn't think he was good enough for her, disapproved of his running a pool hall. Actually the poor fellow just sort of fell into it. He had to support his mother and sisters for so many years, started when he was just a kid sweeping floors in there after school for twenty-five cents a week. The owner took a liking to him. Gradually turned the business over to him. Life's funny, isn't it? So much is chance."

But back to our fancy dinner. I felt very special walking into the elegant hotel dining room, where we were shown to a table right by a window with a view of the city. We watched as dusk fell over San Francisco and the gas streetlights winked on. The table was covered with satiny white linen, with big damask napkins folded to look like huge white butterflies. In the center of the table was a bud vase holding a single perfect rose.

A waiter appeared, handing us menus as long and wide as a six-column lead story, and my eyes nearly popped out of my head as I read it! A selection of food that could have been served royalty, I was sure, much of it described in French: *Consomme Fleury* or deviled crabs a la Creole were offered as a first course; a choice of fish or roast lamb with mint sauce or Ragout of filet beef, *a la Bordelaise,* as a second; and there were several choices of salads and vegetables, and a list of desserts that made the choice difficult — *Strawberry Bavaroise, Gateaux a la Royale,* lemon ice cream. After much indecision and whispering, we settled on the same order, which made it easier for Dan to deal with the aloof waiter.

But nothing dampened our pleasure and we ate, talked, enjoyed everything. I don't know how much our dinner cost and did not dare ask Dan as we left. Since he suggested a walk while our dinner settled, I gathered he was not sure he had enough left to take me home in a cab, so I readily agreed that it was a good idea.

Anyway, it gave us more time together. Funny, but we never ran out of things to talk about this whole long day.

As we said good night, Dan squeezed both my hands and said, "Kit, I can't remember when I've had such a good time! Thanks!"

"Well, thank you, Dan," I said, adding, "— and Uncle Ned!"

"How about your next day off?" he asked.

My heart seemed to swell up into my throat, and I could hardly answer. Was it really happening? Dan Brooks wanting to be with *me?*

"Fine," I managed to say, and Dan was off and running to catch the last trolley to the hospital in time to go on duty.

Dear Jamie and Gwynny,

I haven't written in a long time since I've been so busy at work, too tired when I get in at night, and my days off? Well, I've been spending almost every one with Dan. We've explored San Francisco from top to bottom and now have our own special places we like to go, our favorite restaurants. Mostly we walk out along the beach. Like all midwesterners, we're fascinated by the ocean. We also go to Golden Gate Park, sometimes picnic on the grassy knoll, and talk and talk about everything — Dan's work, my job, my writing, his plans. We've even talked some about our families. I've told him all about you two, how I've never really gotten over losing track of you, missing you, and he's told me about his funny, mixed-up life.

His grandmother is dead now and one of his aunts got married, which I know would surprise a lot of people, especially Toddy and Laurel. We always thought of Dan's aunts as typical "old maids," but Leatrice up and married and took off to live in Oregon, Dan says. His other aunt kept the house for a while, then went to live with his mother in Dayton, Ohio. So he really has no more family than I do. It makes you feel closer to someone the more you know about them, about their childhood. We've had so many of the same experiences, the same feelings about — well, being different from other people we knew growing up. Of course, Laurel and Toddy were "Orphan Train" children, too, but their lives were not like mine and Dan's.

He plans to go back to Meadowridge when he finishes. That's the only thing we don't agree on. Somehow I feel San Francisco is where I'm supposed to be, supposed to stay. I don't know exactly why or for how long, but I can't see going back to Meadowridge right now.

Dear Jamie and Gwynny,

The most exciting thing happened today! Leo Hoffman, the entertainment columnist, came by my little cubicle at the paper and put an envelope down on my desk.

"What's this, Leo?" I called after him when he began to walk away.

"Open it and see." He grinned and the cigar he's always chewing on moved from one side of his mouth to the other.

I did and nearly let out a yelp of surprise. Inside were two tickets to the opera! The San Francisco Opera House! For the opening performance of Bizet's *Carmen*, starring the internationally famous Enrico Caruso!

"Oh, Leo, thank you! Why *me?*"

He wrinkled his face into something that looked exactly like one of those rubber dolls you can squeeze into all sorts of contortions, then rubbed his balding head and muttered, "Heard you liked music. Heard you were a good kid! What difference does it make *why?* You've got the tickets, haven't you? Go and enjoy!" he snarled and walked away.

I can hardly believe my luck! The city has been buzzing with excited anticipation ever since Caruso's appearance was announced. He'd already provided the reporters who had met him on his arrival with colorful copy. I've heard the world-renowned tenor travels in a private railway car, lavishly furnished with Oriental rugs and a piano, with his own valet and cook.

The opening of the opera is always one of the most gala events of the San Francisco social season, attended by anyone who *is* anybody in society, the ladies gowned in satin, ermines and glittering with jewels.

What a thrill it will be to be an observer, even if from the third balcony. I can't wait to tell Dan and of course, invite him to use the other ticket!

20

Kit turned in her day's copy. Then, sweeping all her notes, clippings, pencils, notebooks, paper clips, odds and ends of the sort that accumulate on most reporters' desks into the drawer, she shoved it closed, locked it, and ran down the steps and out the door of the newspaper building into the April sunshine.

Spring had come suddenly to San Francisco, and Kit felt the welcome warmth of the sun on her shoulders and back as she strolled along. She could not stop smiling every time she thought of the opera tickets and how happy Dan would be when he got the message she had left for him at the hospital. It would be a first experience for both of them, for she knew Dan had never attended the opera either. That they were actually to hear with their own ears the glorious voice that had sung for kings and emperors and sultans seemed too much to believe, and Kit's irrepressible smile appeared again.

Today every person she passed on the street seemed happy, too. Maybe it was the weather — "What is so rare as an *April* day," she misquoted giddily. "If ever there come perfect days," *this* was it.

Everything delighted her — the colorful displays in the store windows she passed, the flower vendors' stalls on nearly every corner, bright with spring flowers. She felt as buoyant as a birthday balloon.

Then, as she was passing a milliner's shop, Kit stopped short. Her heart gave a little leap of recognition. There *it* was in the window, as if just waiting for her, whispering, "Buy me, buy me!" She moved closer and leaned against the glass to get a better look.

It was the most beautiful hat Kit had ever seen. Fashioned of soft, pliant pale blue straw, the crown was wrapped with pleated lavender satin ribbon. Nestled in the curve of the brim was a cluster of deep purple silk violets.

Kit's hands tightened on her handbag. Inside was her week's paycheck. Mentally she ticked off the bills she had intended to pay with this week's wages.

The price tag on the hat was turned over. A clever device to lure the interested buyer inside, she thought.

Kit hesitated, her common sense vying with pure feminine desire. Just once to do something impulsive, foolish was tempting. She had never had such a hat. In fact, she had never had many really pretty things. She thought of the evening ahead with Dan — going to the Opera House, hearing Caruso sing the part of Don Jose — a once-in-a-lifetime treat. Surely such a momentous event deserved something special to wear. Kit resisted only a split-second more, then with a small, defiant toss of her head, she opened the door of the shop and went inside.

Twenty minutes later she emerged and, although her heart was racing, the smile was in place. The hat was safely nestled in layers of tissue paper in the smart, round hatbox that bore the proud name of the exclusive millinery establishment.

"In for a penny, in for a pound," Kit thought rashly as she walked further down the street. Once her paycheck had been cashed, something reckless was loosed in Kit. Next she stopped and bought herself a pair of lavender gloves and a lace jabot to wear with her good gray suit. *Real* Chinese lace. Kit had never forgotten Miss Cady's admonition about lace. In the wake of all this extravagance, her pulses were pounding, but before rushing home and out of temptation's way, she made one more stop. A perfumery shop. Immediately her senses were soothed by a hundred assorted fragrances. Here, under the soft-voiced clerk's dulcet persuasion, she purchased a bar of creamy scented soap, some glycerine and rose water for her complexion, some lavender Eau de Cologne.

When Kit left this last shop, she felt she should, by all rights, be burdened with guilt. Instead, she felt lighthearted and entirely pleased with herself.

It was going to be an extraordinary night, a wonderful night, one she was sure she would always remember, a date she would be able to mark on her calendar as a memorable one — April 17,1906.

At two hours past midnight on April 18, Kit climbed wearily into bed, the music of *Carmen* still playing in her ears. Tired as she was, she was much too stimulated to go right to sleep. Scenes of the glittering opera house marched in her mind — the promenade of extravagantly gowned women escorted by men in elegant evening clothes up the sweeping staircase, the magnificence of the gilded boxes where the very wealthy sat, settling their furs and capes, fluttering beaded fans, acknowledging other box-holders with nods and bows and smiles, ignoring everyone else.

Kit had observed every detail, thrilling to the experience while making mental notes to include in her letter to Jamie and Gwynny.

As people took their places, there had been a palpable excitement, permeating the opera house from the lofty heights of the tiers of balconies down to the main floor. An air of anticipation rippled through the entire building as the houselights dimmed. Then a hush fell over the audience and there was only a discreet muffled cough and a rustling of programs as people settled down to enjoy the performance. As Bizet's thrilling overture rose from the orchestra pit, the footlights came up, the music swelled, the heavy velvet curtain lifted, and the gaily costumed chorus of singing girls from the cigarette factory danced onto the stage.

The whole evening had been unforgettable. Not least of it all had been the fact that Kit had been there with Dan. He had not known the story of the opera until Kit told it to him, but he seemed to enjoy the color of the production, the glorious music and singing as much as she.

Afterward they had gone to supper, although not one of the lavish champagne and lobster affairs being served the "haute societe" opera-goers of San Francisco at the luxurious St. Francis or Palace Hotel. They dined, instead, at one of their favorite small North Beach restaurants, where they ate pasta with a creamy clam sauce and crusty sourdough bread and discussed every scene of the opera, exchanging impressions and comparing reactions.

Very much later, when the waiters were yawning discreetly and most of the occupants of the other tables had long since disappeared, Dan had walked Kit to her boardinghouse. She had been distressed by the lateness of the hour, knowing he had to go on duty at seven.

"Don't!" he told her firmly. "It was worth it, every minute. It was wonderful. Imagine having lived twenty-six years and never having seen an opera! If I'd known —" he paused. "You know, Kit, you've introduced me to so many experiences I might have missed — authors whose books you recommended to me when you worked at the library, poetry, music, now opera! If it hadn't been for you, well, science and medicine can give a person a kind of dry, narrow-minded —" he paused, searching for the right word.

"Monotony?" she suggested, smiling.

"Exactly!"

They were quiet for a minute, then Dan leaned down and kissed Kit lightly.

"Thanks, Kit, it was one of the greatest evenings of my life."

Taken by surprise, Kit could only stare at him.

Dan grinned and added, "I meant to tell you before. That's the dandiest hat I've ever seen."

Kit stood watching Dan start back down the hill, hands in his pocket, whistling Don Jose's aria. Then, dreamily Kit climbed the stairs to her room, thinking it had all been more than worth it indeed, even if she had to go without lunch for the rest of the week!

Once inside her room, she halted in front of the mirror and tilted her head from one side to the other, admiring her hat from every angle. Then she shook her head at her own image and scolded, "Oh, Kit Ternan, you are an idiot!"

She waltzed around the room, spinning and spinning, flinging her clothes here and there as she undressed. Leaving her hat on till the very last, she took it off and placed it carefully on the bureau where she could see it from the bed. She was still smiling at Dan's remark when, before putting out her lamp, she gave it a last fond glance and drifted off to sleep.

The next thing she knew, she was startled

awake by a violent movement. Her bed was rocking as if shaken by a giant fist. She sat up, clinging to the sides of the mattress as the deep, rolling sensation continued.

Outside, she could hear dogs barking, and a rumbling as the whole house seemed to roll. Creaking, groaning, cracking, splintering, crumbling noises surrounded her as she gripped the edge of the bed. She felt like screaming, but nothing came out of her throat as she held on for dear life.

There were sounds of crockery falling, glass breaking, heavy objects crashing to the floor all around her. Her pitcher and washbowl slid off the washstand and broke, pouring water all over. Her toilet articles fell in a jumble, followed by the bureau itself, pitching forward. As the drawers were thrust out, their contents spilled out onto the floor.

The roaring sound seemed to go on forever. Then came one final rough jolt, when the very walls seemed to shudder. Finally everything quivered to a halt and a dreadful silence descended.

Was this the end of the world?

For an endless few minutes, Kit huddled in bed, shivering, straining to listen, braced for what might come next. Then slowly she moved over to the side of the bed and swung her legs over. Her bare feet touched the scatter rug. Still holding onto the bed, she gingerly tested her weight on the floor that tilted crazily. It seemed stable enough. Cautiously she stood up, grabbed her clothes from where she had tossed them on the nearby chair, thankful now she had been too tired to hang them up or put them away the night before. The chest of drawers was upended. Breathing hard, she quickly dragged her nightie over her head and pulled on her underclothes. Her fingers shook so that she fumbled with buttons and hooks. She never knew how, but somehow she managed to get dressed.

Whatever had happened she had to get out, see what it was. She crept over to the window and saw people, in wrappers and robes, pouring out of buildings on both sides of the street. They were shouting and calling to each other. "Earthquake! Earthquake!" Everyone looked as frightened as Kit felt, as though any minute the earth would start moving again.

Kit could hear voices and cries and rushing feet in the hall outside her room. She went to the door and tried to open it. However, the earthquake had twisted the doorframe so that the door was stuck. She could not budge it. She tugged frantically, pulling the knob in vain. With a groan of frustration, she ran back to the open window. Leaning on the sill, she looked down. Could she possibly climb out onto the roof, slide down to the ledge above the porch that fronted the house? Maybe let herself down to the porch railing and to the ground?

The ground was a very long way. Feeling dizzy, she gripped the sill to steady herself Her heart was hammering, but she knew she had to get out or else be trapped in the house if another quake hit. Kit had heard that sometimes the aftershocks were as bad as the first, and this three-story frame house, teetering as it was on the edge of the hill, had never seemed very substantial to her. She felt faint and closed her eyes, murmuring, "Oh, God, help me!"

Then into her mind came verses she had memorized in Sunday school. Gratefully she repeated them to herself now: " 'Fear not, for I am with thee; be not dismayed, for I am thy God. I will strengthen thee, yes, I will help thee. I will uphold thee with My righteous right hand.' Thank you, Lord!" she whispered breathlessly and grabbed her shoes, tied them by their laces around her neck, scooped up her notebook, stuffed it into her handbag, and started out the window.

As she perched on the sill ready to swing herself around, she saw the hat! Her beautiful hat with its satin ribbons and bunch of violets! She hesitated a split-second. It was ridiculous, she knew, but she could not leave it when this building itself might topple any minute. She scrambled back into the room, grabbed it, and jammed it on over her sleep-tousled hair.

The straps of her handbag hung on her arm as she crawled over the roof to the edge. It was then someone in the crowd below looked up and saw her.

"Wait a minute, lady!" a man hollered up to her. "Don't try to climb down by yourself!"

"Thank God!" murmured Kit, and she clung there, trying not to panic as the man hurried over to stand directly below her.

"It's a pretty good drop," he yelled, holding up his arms. "So try to lower yourself slowly, and I'll catch you."

Kit prayed a desperate prayer and then, still hanging on to the gutter with one hand, she lowered herself, let go and fell forward. Her shoes struck her in the mouth as she did so, and she cried out just as she felt strong hands grasp her around her waist. Her weight made the man stagger and sent them both sprawling on the grass, but at least she was safely out of the house.

"Thank you!" she said breathlessly as the man got to his feet, stretched out a hand to pull her up. "That was very brave of you."

"You're a plucky girl."

Standing there in her bare feet in the chill foggy morning, Kit's journalistic instincts surfaced. She dug in her handbag for her notebook and asked, "Could I have your name?"

Even as she scribbled it down and listened to the man telling his *own* earthquake story, something rang in Kit's head. It was Clem's voice, saying, "It's being in the right place at the right time. If you're lucky, you'll recognize it when you're on to a *big* story."

This was the *big story!* Kit knew, and she was right here in the midst of it.

She sat down on the listing steps of the house and, as discreetly as possible, put on her stockings and shoes. Then she took out the small brush she kept in her handbag and swept it through her hair, pinning it up under the inappropriate hat. This was the story of the century, something told her. Writing it would give her unassailable credentials as a journalist.

As the fog lifted, people reacted in surprising ways. An almost carnival atmosphere emerged from the dark terror of the frightening moments before daylight. Then messages began to filter in from other parts of the city — alarming reports of whole blocks collapsing, taking with them buildings full of sleeping occupants, bodies trapped in the suffocating wreckage.

Rumors began to circulate. One horrifying possibility was that the whole of downtown San Francisco had disappeared. Kit wondered about the newspaper building. It was old, with many additions as it had expanded. She thought of the press room with its huge, heavy machinery, and the shelves and shelves of lead typefaces. So near Market Street, that building must have suffered severe damage. And if the composing room was gone, there would be no paper.

Still, she kept on taking notes, moving among the crowd as more and more people from other stricken areas joined the ranks of the hilltop neighborhood. Kit sensed that just under the surface panic simmered as dazed persons wandered through, asking about friends and family members they could not locate. The day became an endless procession of the homeless, dragging their possessions from what remained of the rubble of their houses, searching for a place to stay.

Military personnel from Golden Gate

Fort rode in on horseback, taking charge, warning people not to try to go back into the buildings until they were declared safe, offering to escort any who desired shelter to the fort, which was being readied for the refugees.

As it began to grow dark, a strange red glow appeared in the sky. Murmurs rippled through the crowd as people speculated on its cause. Then a kind of unified gasp was heard as word came back that San Francisco was on fire! Fire, started by broken gas mains, devouring the city — house by house, street by street, entire blocks and buildings! Worse still, because of the damage done to water pipes by the quake, there was no water to fight it! San Francisco was doomed!

Angry discussions erupted, people blaming the unknown idiot of an engineer who had planned the city's water supply lines across the path of the San Andreas Fault! Rage, incredulity, fear, panic — every conceivable emotion surfaced as the truth of their predicament dawned on the populace. Then, all emotion spent, they settled in to wait it out — a silence broken only by the occasional cry of a baby, a muffled sob, hushed exclamations of despair.

Hours passed. Kit would try to recall

from her notes just what happened then. As it was, she kept working — asking questions, jotting down answers, seeking information from every source she could find. When her stub of a pencil became blunt, she borrowed another and wrote on.

Suddenly Kit heard another sound — a familiar sound no less terrifying because it reminded her of many a Fourth of July in Meadowridge. Like the burst of cherry bombs or fireworks on display came a series of explosions. Rumors spread as fast as the raging fire. Some said the military arsenal had blown up. Others denied it, saying the firemen were dynamiting the fire breaks. And since no one knew for sure, a general anxiety fell over the crowd, as heavy as the pall of smoke now shrouding the city.

As the late afternoon fog began to roll in from the Bay, it hung over the hills and made its usual slow descent, adding its unique gloom. In the dark of early evening the eerie wail of foghorns seemed to be sounding a dirge of destruction.

Here and there small clusters of people settled down to spend the night. Most people had not thought to bring food with them when they fled their houses in panic. As a few small campfires were lighted, a sense of camaraderie moved people to share what little they had. They exchanged their stories and their concerns as well, trying to support what small hope still lingered in worried hearts. Some expressed their anxiety for missing family members, and Kit wondered with a sharp pang where Dan was and if he had survived!

With thousands injured, many still buried in the rubble of demolished buildings, rescue teams worked steadily to bring relief, while all available medical personnel was recruited, doctors and nurses giving aid everywhere. Hospital patients were evacuated and taken to the military compound.

Throughout the long night, the fire swept on like a great dragon, scorching section after section of the city in its hot breath. Embarcadero bluejackets manned pumps with water from the Bay, trying desperately to quench the fire's insatiable thirst.

Her pencil worn to a nub, her body and mind exhausted, Kit shivered in the dampness, more from nerves than from the chill of the night air. So much of what she had seen, heard, experienced this long day could not be immediately recalled. Her emotions seemed deadened, too. A catastrophe of this magnitude was almost incomprehensible, and Kit knew she would have to sort out all the facts, organize her impressions, give herself time to translate this tragedy in terms of human suffering.

Even in her numbed condition Kit slowly began to form her lead. Eventually, she realized, there would be hundreds of stories filed. To be printed hers would have to be outstanding. She needed something dramatic —

"The Ferry Building at the foot of Market Street remained gleaming white among charred telephone poles, cracked cement, piles of rubble, the hands of the clock on its side eerily stopped at exactly 5:15 A.M., the time the earthquake struck — a literal Phoenix rising out of the ashes of a once beautiful city."

As police and military patrolled the streets, word went out that looters were being shot on sight. Rumor or not, it was terrifying for those who had businesses downtown or houses out of which they had rushed, bringing nothing with them but the clothes on their backs.

Kit heard that the big downtown hospital, where Dan was a resident physician, had been hit hard, and rescue parties were trying to find and bring out those who had been injured or trapped in the wreckage. As they dusted off the victims — doctors and nurses and even a few patients — who had suffered nothing more than a severe shaking, these in turn joined the rescue effort. Once out of the damaged building, the hospitalized ill and injured must be transported to a safe location, and the military hospital at the Presidio was designated.

If Dan had survived — and right now she couldn't let herself imagine the alternative — Kit knew he would be among those brave souls who, with no thought for their own safety, would be trying to save others.

Similar acts of unselfish bravery were being repeated all over the city.

As night came on, hundreds of homeless who had not elected to go to the fort were being herded to Golden Gate Park, where tents were already being erected as a temporary shelter.

Kit was undecided as to just what to do when she ran into Nelly Armstrong, a friend from the newspaper, and learned from her that the building itself had been destroyed. They held on to each other, seeing the horror of what had happened reflected in each other's white faces. Kit was relieved to learn messages were being sent over the Postal wire, and reporters were filing their stories from Oakland.

Relief trains had already left Los Angeles with medical supplies, doctors and nurses on their way to help the devastated city. Soup kitchens were being set up to feed the hundreds of people now left without kitchens of their own, food or money to buy it.

Nelly told Kit that her own place, a small one-story house, had somehow managed to escape total disaster. The damage consisted mostly of broken windows, smashed crockery, a few pictures jounced off the walls. She invited Kit to stay with her until Kit could find out if the rooming house would be declared habitable again or at least until she could go back and collect her things.

Gratefully, Kit accepted, and it was sitting at Nelly's kitchen table that Kit began to write the earthquake story that would bring startling changes in her life.

EXCLUSIVE TO *MEADOWRIDGE MONITOR*

From: Kathleen Ternan   Date line: San Francisco, April 18, 1906

At 5:15 A.M. in the gray, foggy dawn of this April morning, disaster struck the beautiful city by the Bay, San Francisco, California. Citizens were awakened, roused out of sound sleep by a terrible rumbling noise followed by a series of strong, jolting shocks that wrought catastrophic damage on streets and buildings, as well as causing death and injuries. As buildings toppled and walls crumbled, falling bricks and beams smashed into sidewalks, and huge craters opened in the streets. Telephone and telegraph poles came crashing down, splintering in a tangle of wires. No one realized it at first, but this would serve to cut the city off from all communication with the outside world for a matter of hours.

Unless you saw it yourself, it would be impossible to image the extent of Nature's destruction on this city.

The days that followed the earthquake were formless. A heavy curtain, like that of the city's smoke, hung over the people; people who walked like robots, people who looked as if they were in some kind of trance.

Every day Kit ventured out gathering more material for her earthquake report. It was the stories of individuals that interested her most. There were many stories of missing family members and happier ones of re-unions. Over and over Kit heard people say, "This kind of thing changes your priorities," "You learn what's important." Bankers stood in food lines with carpenters, housemaids with their mistresses. A kind of macabre joke, repeated often, was "An earthquake is a great leveler." Even with all the confusion and the dreadful destruction, the human spirit proved again and again to be triumphant, great acts of courage done on behalf of strangers, kindnesses rendered, generosity extended.

She knew many fine reporters were writing other kinds of stories — descriptions of the fires, the destruction of well-known mansions, hotels, restaurants and commercial buildings, so Kit concentrated on what was known in the trade as "human interest" stories. And there was no lack of those.

By Friday the fires were pretty well under control. Only smoldering pockets remained here and there, and over all the fine cindery dust and a lingering pall of smoke. Kit had set out early that morning, hoping her PRESS card might get her past the barriers to downtown so that she could see for herself what remained of the once-proud business section, see the skeletons of the luxurious mansions.

She was in the process of convincing one of the policemen to let her through when she heard someone hoarsely shouting her name.

"Kit! Kit Ternan!"

She whirled around and saw Dan, gray-faced, haggard, hollow-eyed, his hair rumpled, wearing a torn, stained, once-white medical jacket over a soiled shirt. He looked as though he had not slept in days, and his stride was slow even as he tried to hurry toward her.

Lifting her skirts over the fallen debris, Kit ran to meet him. In the middle of the ruined street, they hugged, laughing hysterically.

"Oh, Dan, I'm so *glad* to see you!"

"Kit, Kit, I was so worried about you!"

As their words tumbled over each other, they shared scraps of information about what had transpired since they had parted the night of the opera.

"That all seems a hundred years ago!" Kit shook her head in disbelief.

"Another lifetime," agreed Dan. "Everything is gone, Kit. So many hurt, so many dead." His own fiery trial had etched new lines of strength and compassion about Dan's eyes and mouth.

"I know. It's been like a bad dream."

"A nightmare," Dan said solemnly. "I came looking for you, Kit, hoping you'd be in the vicinity of your boardinghouse. When you weren't there, I almost went wild —"

Quickly Kit told him where she was staying.

"I've been ordered to get some sleep," Dan said at last. "We're quartered in the barracks at the Presidio. Then I go back on duty. But I wanted to make sure you were safe before I —" Dan broke off and touched the brim of Kit's hat. He smiled down at her, an amused twinkle glimmering in his tired eyes. "I see you're still attached to your hat!"

Kit laughed, too. She had almost forgotten her beautiful violet-trimmed hat, now much the worse for wear.

Dan put both his hands on either side of her face, then unexpectedly bent down and kissed her on the mouth.

"I still say it's one of the dandiest hats I've ever seen," he said softly.

A month later, Dan was sitting in Nelly Armstrong's kitchen across from Kit, reading one of her articles published about the earthquake and its aftermath. Dan had not seen all the articles, so when he came over on his regular day off to see her at Nelly's, where she was still staying, Kit had shown him her tear-sheets.

"It's good, Kit, really good." Dan looked up from the paper he was holding. "You're quite a writer."

Kit felt a warm flush rise into her cheeks, wash over her face and throat under his admiring glance. She got up and went over to the stove and, lifting the coffeepot, asked, "More?"

Dan shoved his mug toward her and she refilled it.

"Wait until I tell you some exciting news, Dan. It seems my series on the earthquake — the little incidents and interviews I did with people — were picked up by newspapers back East as well. And guess what? I've been offered a chance to write for a woman's magazine. The editor of *Woman's Hearth and Home* wrote to me, asked me if I'd be interested in doing a series of articles for them. She said, *and* I quote —" Kit's voice took on a dramatic tone — " 'We'd like to see the same kind of heart-tugging, human interest type stories you did on your series on the San Francisco earthquake.' " Here Kit struck a Napoleonic pose. "I think at last my career is taking off."

"Congratulations, Kit!" Dan said heartily. "That *is* good news! You'll have no trouble getting your old job back at the *Monitor*." He grinned. "You're a celebrity in Meadowridge now."

Kit looked puzzled as she sat back down and spooned sugar into her coffee.

"But I have no plans to get my old job back, Dan."

He reached across the table and his hand closed over hers. Looking at her steadily, he said, "Let's go home, Kit."

She stared at him blankly.

"Dr. Woodward's contacted me again, wants me to join his practice," Dan went on. "He's made me a generous offer, Kit. You know I always wanted to be a country doctor, and this would mean stepping into an established practice. Most of all, I'd be working with a man I like and admire. It's a great opportunity."

Kit struggled with several conflicting emotions. Her mouth suddenly dry, she took a swallow of coffee. "That's wonderful, Dan. I'm happy for you."

"Didn't you hear what I said, Kit?" He pressed the hand he was holding. "I said, let's go home, meaning *you and I* . . . together!"

"I don't understand —" she said haltingly.

"Don't you realize I've fallen in love with you, Kit? I think I've actually loved you for a long time, only I didn't know it. I want us to get married and go back to Meadowridge together."

Kit felt her pulse begin a staccato beat.

Dan regarded her with a mixture of amusement and affection. "You really didn't know I loved you, did you?" His tone was quizzical.

She shook her head. "I always thought we were just — good friends."

"That's the best kind of love, Kit, to begin as good friends." He was smiling, but his eyes were serious as he searched hers for some idea of what she was thinking, feeling. "So, what do you say?"

Longing for him swept through Kit like a strong Bay wind. Could it really be true? Dan, whom she had long ago given up as an impossible dream, offering her his love and life?

As she gazed at him in a kind of stunned bewilderment, he reached for both of her hands and covered them in a strong clasp.

"Kit, you're everything I want in a woman. You're brave and kind and smart and compassionate . . . and beautiful. I want you to share my life."

Kit swallowed hard, her heart pumping so loudly she was certain it must be audible to Dan's well-trained ear, even without a stethoscope. She struggled to formulate the question she dreaded asking.

"What is it, Kit? Something's troubling you," Dan said, looking anxious. "Maybe being a country doctor's wife isn't your cup of tea."

"No, Dan, it isn't that — although I never really thought about it. But it isn't that at all."

She paused, then taking a deep breath, she made the plunge. "What about Laurel, Dan? I know you've always loved her."

A slight shadow darkened Dan's eyes for a moment before he answered. "I did love Laurel, I *do* love her, and I'll always love her. But, Kit, I loved her as a boy loves a sweet young girl, with all those first youthful feelings he thinks will last forever. Of course they don't, and Laurel never loved *me* like that." He hesitated. "Loving Laurel was part of growing up. She is part of my life. Just as you have always been a part of my life, Kit." He paused and, looking at her intently, went on, "But over these past months this feeling for you has been growing until I realized it was there all the time, like a beautiful seed planted that just needed time, exposure, tending, to mature into what it is now — a *man's* love for the woman he wants to spend the rest of his life with.

"I know the difference now. I believe I know what real love is — wanting someone to be with you always, knowing you're understood, knowing that person wants all the things you want for yourself." He paused. "But how can I convince you, Kit, that my feelings for you are real, that I love you, that I want to marry you?"

Kit returned his anxious look, her eyes

shining with astonished happiness. "I *do* believe you, Dan. And I'm honored that you . . . care for me that way. But . . . I don't know. I don't know whether I'm ready . . . I don't know if I want to go back to Meadowridge. You see, it took so long, and I worked so hard to get away, to get a foothold in what I want to do." She halted, then continued slowly, "Because you see, Dan, I *do* want to be a writer, and I don't know if I can marry you and write too."

"But a writer can write anywhere."

"It's not just the place, Dan. It's the time, the energy, the dedication necessary to become a really *good* writer. My heart would be divided. I just don't know if I can —"

"You don't have to give me an answer right away, Kit. I don't finish at the hospital until August, and Dr. Woodward is not expecting me until September." Dan got up, came around the table, and gently drew her up and into his arms. "Just please don't say no."

His touch kindled the long-banked flame of her feelings for him, and they sprang alive within her. Kit leaned against him, and it was a beautiful, safe feeling. As she felt the strength of his arms about her, she was surprised at how natural it felt to be there.

Yet how was it possible to be handed what

you had always thought would be your heart's desire and then, when it was offered, not be sure?

"It's an important decision, Dan," she murmured.

"I know. Take all the time you need, Kit. I'm not going to stop loving you."

21

Throughout the next busy months San Francisco vigorously set about rebuilding. The city seemed to have found a new energy, a new spirit, a kind of proud defiance in showing the world it could come back from the brink of annihilation bigger, stronger, more beautiful than ever.

Everywhere in the city could be seen signs of construction. People filled the streets, still under repair, going about their business with renewed purpose. Flower vendors were back at their corners, banks and stores were open for business, restaurants served their customers as if April 18 had been just another day.

The lifeblood of the city throbbed, coursing through every artery of its commerce and industry. Kit was both gratified and disturbed by all this progress. The accelerated pace proved a distraction from the concentration needed for her new writing assignment. Not only that, but night after night she lay awake, pondering the decision for which Dan was patiently waiting before he left for Meadowridge at the end of August.

There was a deep longing in Kit to be cherished, cared for and sheltered by the kind of love Dan was offering. But there was also a fierce ambition to make something of herself, to reach some of her long-held goals, to prove that an orphan can achieve in spite of little encouragement, with only sheer determination and dogged persistence.

Could she have both? Kit tossed and turned endlessly, trying to solve those demanding questions. In her heart, she believed God *had* given her the gift of expressing thoughts and feelings, describing events and people and she had worked hard to develop that gift. She was on the brink of something now that she could not bring herself to give up.

On one of those sleepless nights, a compelling idea for a series of articles came to Kit that brought her wide awake. She realized she had been subconsciously thinking about it for a long time. Now, it seemed the perfect time to write it.

When Kit discussed it with Dan, he encouraged her to go ahead.

"I know it will touch a lot of people, Kit. It's your story. No one else can tell it the way you can. You'll be writing it for Toddy and Laurel and all the children like you three, who were on the Orphan Train."

Night after night, with the light from the oil lamp burning glow, Kit emptied her heart through her pen, letting all of it flow through her — the good and bad, the joy and sorrow, the pleasure and pain.

Little Lost Family
by Kathleen Ternan
Within each human heart is a deep longing for a place to belong, not one that must be earned or won or demanded, but is one's right by birth. If that birthright is denied through whatever of circumstance, there is forever a void in that life that nothing else can ever fill.

Twenty years ago in Boston, Massachusetts, this happened to my small brother and sister and me and we became a "little lost family" —

Writing of her experiences as an abandoned child, the remembered feelings of sadness and grief almost overwhelmed her. But Kit wrote on and as she did, allowing her feelings to emerge, her heart was opened to a new understanding, a gentleness, a compassionate understanding for the young, grief-stricken, widowed father who had left the three of them at Greystone Orphanage.

Something else happened during the writing of this article. Until then, Kit had not realized how much she had suppressed, not daring to risk feeling her pain and loss.

At first she thought she might have said too much, revealed too much, opened her inner self too much, knowing this piece would be read by strangers. And yet, after she had put it aside for a week or more, then reread it, Kit discovered a marvelous truth. There was healing power in her creative words — healing for others, for *herself*. It was with a sense of relief that Kit did the final editing and then sent it off to *Woman's Hearth and Home*.

The summer passed swiftly and then it was time for Dan to leave. Reluctantly Kit let him go without an answer.

"I'm willing to wait, Kit," he told her as he kissed her goodbye.

Later Kit wrote in her journal, "How can a city filled with people, with noise and endless activity, be such a lonely place because one person is missing?"

She tried to work hard at the paper during the day so that she would be tired enough to sleep at night. But most nights she stayed up writing. She was like a person possessed, filling page after page with stories, many of them near-forgotten incidents from her childhood.

Every day she checked her mailbox hopefully for a response to her submission to *Woman's Hearth and Home*. Weeks went by, each one seeming longer than the last. She missed Dan more than she had imagined possible and she fretted anxiously about the story she had submitted. Maybe it had been too personal, too sad, oversentimentalized? Maybe she should stick to straight reporting.

Then one day she found a long envelope in her box with the magazine's letterhead. With trembling hands Kit opened it. A check was enclosed. The amount was more than she had expected, twice as much as she had received for her "earthquake" story, and a letter from the editor that Kit read with ever-mounting excitement.

Dear Miss Ternan,

We are impressed with your latest submission, "Little Lost Family," the account of your experiences as an Orphan Train rider. All members of our editorial staff have read it and, I must tell you, it evoked many a heartfelt tear. At our monthly meeting it was unanimously decided to feature this article as the lead story in our December issue — always a popular one with a larger than average readership. I think your story will bring a warm response from our readers.

We are looking forward to having you as a regular contributor to our magazine and hope you will be submitting many more of this type of heart-warming article.

Kit was elated. But with no one to share this exciting news, her joy soon evaporated and the old self-doubts resurfaced.

That night as Kit lay in bed, she was haunted by old memories — nights of lying in the narrow cot in the dormitory at Greystone Orphanage when she felt so abandoned, the nights on the Orphan Train roaring across the dark prairie when she was frightened of what was going to happen to her, wondering if anyone would ever really care about her, and those long nights up in her loft room at the Hansen farm when she would stare into the dark, fighting the fear and loneliness.

It's your own fault, she admonished herself. *You could have gone back to Meadowridge with Dan. Right now you could be in his arms, warm, safe, protected — loved!*

What good was even long-worked — for

success if there was no one to share it?

Kit received a complimentary issue of the December *Woman's Hearth and Home* and stared at it, unbelieving. An illustration of a heartbreaking trio of children who looked nothing like her, Jamie, or Gwynny accompanied the article, but even that didn't matter. There was her name, KATHLEEN TERNAN, printed in bold letters in a nationally published periodical!

Kit celebrated Christmas with Nelly and some of the other people from the newspaper who lived too far to go home for the short holiday. Dan sent her a leather writing portfolio, one that could be placed comfortably on her lap. In the enclosed card, he had written, "Just to remind you that it's possible to write *anywhere,* even on a train to Meadowridge!"

Kit's usual optimism was lacking as the New Year was announced by church bells and whistles piercing the foggy midnight. She had turned down an invitation to a party and spent the evening curled up in bed writing in her journal, wondering what 1907 would hold for her.

At the end of January she received a letter from Eleanor Hargrove, the editor of *Woman's Hearth and Home.* In it she told Kit the response to "Little Lost Family" had been staggering. The magazine had been deluged with letters asking for reprints, and she enclosed an additional check, asking permission to comply with their readers' requests.

Miss Hargrove also said the magazine was forwarding, under separate cover, letters that had been addressed personally to the author and that Kit should be receiving them soon. She closed by asking when they could expect another article.

In the same day's mail there was a large manila envelope containing dozens of letters addressed to Kit in care of the magazine. As she read one after the other, Kit had to stop often to wipe her eyes. Then she came upon one envelope whose familiar handwriting and return address surprised her. It was from Miss Cady! The letter began:

I have just read your beautiful story reprinted in our newspaper from *Woman's Hearth and Home*. I have long regretted the circumstances of our parting and blame myself. It was my own pride that dictated you should be an example of my work — my accomplishment. Of course, your success is no such thing! You have succeeded through your own diligent effort, your desire to excel. God has a way of bringing about His purpose in a person's life and I can see you have found the unique place He planned for you and are doing the work He has called you to do. Forgive me for not understanding.

Always your friend,
Millicent Cady

Kit read the letter over twice. Never had anything meant so much to her. The unreconciled friendship with Miss Cady had always been an aching bruise in her heart. If nothing else positive came from her article, this alone was sufficient reward.

But there was more to come. Within a week another letter was forwarded to Kit from the magazine. The envelope was of fine, pale gray, deckle-edged stationery; the handwriting, a cultured script.

When Kit opened it and unfolded the letter, a small photograph fell out. She picked it up and looked at it. It was of a beautiful young woman, dressed in an exquisite wedding veil, her dress embroidered with lace and tiny seed pearls.

Puzzled, Kit began to read:

My dear Miss Ternan,
    You do not know me, but I have just

finished reading your poignant article, "Little Lost Family," in the current issue of *Woman's Hearth and Home* magazine. I was greatly moved. Indeed, almost overcome with emotion. I knew I had to write to you, but I must beg your discretion in the matter I am about to reveal to you.

After ten childless years, my husband and I adopted a beautiful two-year-old baby girl from the Greystone Orphanage. We adored her from the time we set eyes upon her cherubic face, rosy cheeks, big, blue eyes, and masses of ringlets. As I looked upon her that first day, she held out her arms to me, and I clasped her to my heart. It was as if some Higher Power had directed us and we knew instinctively we belonged to each other.

We brought her home and reared her with perfect love and tenderness, seeing that she had every advantage — physical, material, spiritual. She grew up to be a lovely, sweet, talented young lady who never gave us a moment's anxiety and returned the love we lavished upon her.

She has done well in her studies, has a sweet singing voice, and plays the harp. Last year she became engaged to a fine young man, the son of family friends, who has just graduated with a Law Degree and will be joining the distinguished firm of his father and grandfather.

At this point, I must confess, that shortly after the adoption, my husband and I moved to another town where he was to take over the management of a mill, and in this new situation, everyone assumed Gwynny was our own child. We never told her she was adopted. The time never seemed right. She was happy and secure, and the more time that passed, the more we felt it might do great harm if she found out she was not actually our birth child. Let me assure you we consider her such, as if she had been born to us.

But after reading your piece, my heart was deeply touched by *your* suffering, wondering all these years where your baby sister and brother were. That is why I felt compelled to write to tell you about Gwynny.

I have not given you her married name nor where she now resides. I still feel it would be a very disturbing thing for her to find out at this time in her life that she is adopted. I hope and pray you will understand and respect my reasons.

God bless you, my dear. It is my sincere hope that your own life has been as satisfactory as I believe Gwynny would consider hers. You have a God-given gift for expressing the deepest emotions of the human heart and I know you will do a great deal of good with your talent.

The letter was signed only, "A Christian Mother."

The writing blurred before Kit's eyes. Starting from the beginning, she read the letter over again with disbelief. She picked up the small picture, held it, studying each detail. Yes, yes, the eyes, the curls clustered around her forehead, the hint of dimples around the sweetly curved mouth. Even though she was posed with all the demure dignity of a bridal photograph, Kit *could* see the remnants of that precious baby sister.

As she gazed at the face the pain, that had been inside for years, rushed forth in a torrent of tears. But with the pain came release. At last, she knew Gwynny had been safe, beloved, had known a real home, the affectionate care of both parents.

When all Kit's tears were spent, she got out the writing portfolio, dipped her pen in ink and began to write a letter. It was a letter she now felt ready to write. The words came easier than she thought they might. When she came to the end, she signed it, blotted it, got out an envelope and addressed and stamped it. So eager was she that it go out right away that Kit put on her hat and coat and ran to the mailbox at the end of the street. The letter was addressed to Dr. Daniel Brooks of Meadowridge.

22

As the train chugged up the last incline before dipping down into the valley, Kit caught her first sight of Meadowridge in nearly three years. Its rooftops gleaming in the fall sunshine, the spire of the church spiked up into the blue autumn sky, the town lay nestled in rolling hills brilliant with autumn color.

Kit was out of her seat and already moving down the aisle toward the door as the train whistle pierced the air, its engine hissing and its brakes screeching on the rails as it slowed to a stop.

"Meadowridge! Meadowridge, folks!" announced the conductor and Kit's heart leapt. She had a sense of homecoming she had not expected. Then, as she swung down the steps and onto the platform, she saw Dan and tears rushed into her eyes. He was hurrying toward her, long legs covering the distance in record time, waving a bouquet of gold and bronze chrysanthemums.

"Kit, you're here! You're finally here!"

All she could do was nod, her eyes brimming, her heart full.

It wasn't until Dan had given her a hug that nearly left her breathless that Kit saw Dr. and Mrs. Woodward standing behind him at a discreet distance.

As soon as the Woodwards learned of her engagement to Dan and that she was coming home to marry him, Ava had written Kit and told her they would not have it any other way but that she stay with them upon her return to Meadowridge and let them give her wedding.

"You know you are very special to us, as one of the little 'Orphans' who came with our precious Laurel. We always felt you and Toddy were like sisters to Laurel, growing up as you did so close to each other and so much a part of our lives."

Kit read these words over and over, treasuring each one, responding to the love and thoughtfulness that had prompted them.

"Please allow us to do this," Ava had asked.

Dr. Woodward had added his own comments on the invitation by writing Kit to thank her for agreeing to Ava's request.

"Ava looks ten years younger. She is full of excitement and plans. She misses Laurel, as you can imagine, even though both she and Gene have been here for visits. To have a 'daughter' to plan a wedding for has given her a new lease on life. We both are looking forward to your arrival and I want to formally accept with great pleasure the honor you have bestowed on me in asking me to give you away on your great day."

Dr. Woodward had added a P.S. that delighted Kit: "I hope Dan realizes what a lucky young man he is that you have given him your promise to love, cherish and so on! If not, I shall take him aside promptly and inform him of the fact. However, I do not think that will be necessary. He is wandering around Meadowridge with quite an absent expression on his face, frequently forgets things, stares into space, answers in a distracted manner any questions put to him. I would be concerned about him, if I did not know better, for his condition is quite alarming. But having suffered from the same ailment myself thirty-some years ago, I easily recognize that. Dan is love-sick, lonely and anxious. These symptoms will only subside when the only known cure is administered, one Kathleen Ternan arriving in Meadowridge."

Now, they both stood waiting their turn to embrace Kit and welcome her back.

At the Woodwards' house, Kit was warmly greeted by Ella who served them all fresh coffee and cinnamon rolls right out of the oven as they gathered around the dining room table to discuss wedding plans. Dan, who could not seem to take his eyes off Kit, was singularly vague when asked for an opinion or suggestion.

Finally, Dr. Woodward got to his feet and said with a chuckle, "Well, Dan, I think we should leave the ladies to settle the details. You don't seem to be offering much help, and I certainly know nothing about decorations for the church or what kind of punch to serve at the reception. Besides, we have patients to see, my boy."

When the men left, Ava, her arm around Kit's waist, took her upstairs to Laurel's old bedroom to get settled.

"I can't tell you what it means to have you here, Kit," she said giving her a little squeeze. "And I have wonderful news. Laurel is definitely coming for the wedding! We hope she will sing! And we've written to Toddy but she is not sure whether or not she can get time off from her nursing duties. But even if she can't make it, Mrs. Hale insists on having the reception."

"Oh, Mrs. Woodward!" Kit exclaimed. "I never thought — never dreamed — this could all happen!"

Ava looked pleased. "Well, it *is* happening! And no one could deserve it more than you, my dear girl," she said, patting Kit's shoulder affectionately.

Ava left Kit alone in the lovely pink and white bedroom that she had envied in years past. She always loved visiting her friend here where they had shared so many girlish confidences. On the rare occasions she had been allowed by Cora Hansen to stay overnight, Kit secretly used to pretend, before going to sleep, that *this* was *her* room! Now she was to stay here, live in the Woodwards' charming home for two whole weeks before her wedding day.

She walked around, admiring the flowered wallpaper, her hand trailing along the footboard of the polished maple bed, pausing to examine the dainty appointments on the dressing table, the embroidered dresser scarf on the mirrored bureau. Kit recalled that evening, the summer after graduation, when Laurel had met her outside the library after Kit finished work. They had come up here so they could talk in private. That was when Laurel told Kit she was planning to go away. Taken off guard, Kit had asked her, "But how can you leave all this?"

Kit had never forgotten Laurel's reply. "Don't you *really* understand, Kit? Don't you really *know?* Nothing makes up for being an orphan."

Now Kit understood better what Laurel meant. The wounds — of being abandoned, whatever the circumstances, left to fend for oneself in the impersonal atmosphere of an orphanage, daily face the uncertainty of the future — went deep. Maybe they were never really healed, no matter where one was "placed out." The scar tissue remained, and ever after, the pain of that loss surfaced.

Involuntarily Kit shuddered. The worst damage was that she could never quite believe that lasting happiness was possible, that whatever she had might be snatched away without warning. As a result she had learned not to cling to people, not to expect things to last, not to expect happiness. Maybe, that's why it had taken her so long to believe Dan really loved her, wanted her to marry him.

In a rush of gratitude, Kit slipped onto her knees beside the bed, and put her head down upon her clasped hands.

"Dear Lord," she prayed, "help me to trust Your love, Your kindness to me. I know You have brought Dan into my life for a purpose. Make me worthy of his love, help me to accept it and him as Your gracious gift to me. Please help me to become a good wife to him. And, Lord, thank You —"

Before Kit got up from her knees she

whispered the words with which she always closed her prayers. "And bless Gwynny and Jamie, wherever they are."

That evening Dan came for supper and afterwards he and Kit took a long walk along familiar streets in the lingering light of the early autumn evening. Almost unconsciously they ended up at the playground of the old Meadowridge Grammar School. They sat down on adjacent swings and, as they idly pushed back and forth, they talked.

"It seems like a dream to be back here," Kit said. "This brings back so many memories, doesn't it?"

"Yes, but I'd really rather look forward to the future — *our* future. I didn't think it was possible to be this happy," Dan said, twisting his swing around so that he was facing her. "I love you so much, Kit."

His eyes held such tenderness that again Kit felt the start of tears. Trying to make light of them, she said, "I don't know what's wrong with me, doctor, I feel so emotional —"

"Emotions are natural. If we didn't have them, how would we know we're alive?" Dan smiled. Then he got up, held out his hand to her and pulled her to her feet and into his arms. Then, hand in hand, they strolled down toward Meadowridge Park.

It was still light enough to see the ducks skimming on the water at the edge of the lake, making little ripples on its silvery surface.

"I have something for you, Kit." Dan drew a small jewelry box from his coat pocket. He took Kit's hand and placed it in her palm. "Open it."

She looked at him, then down at the rounded velvet box and pressed the spring that lifted the lid. A single luminous pearl shimmered against the deep blue plush lining.

Kit drew in her breath.

"I wasn't sure what kind of engagement ring you might want. Then, when I went to look at them, I knew right away what kind you should have. A pearl seemed to me to represent *you*, Kit — pure, serene, with a deep inner radiance." Dan looked a little embarrassed. "I'm no poet — I wish I could think of something really eloquent to say at a time like this —"

For one who had never owned any jewelry this was the grandest ring she had ever seen, and she felt the surge of tears once more as she took the ring out of the box. "This says it all, Dan. Please, put it on my finger." And she held up her left hand.

"Now, it's official," he said with a grin

when the ring was in place.

Mrs. Danby, a little bent but as sharp-tongued and skilled with a needle as ever, arrived at the Woodwards the following morning, ready to do the final fitting on Kit's wedding dress.

A few weeks before Ava had asked Kit to send her measurements so that Mrs. Danby could get started on her wedding gown, which was to be Ava's gift to her. Knowing she could not possibly afford anything as lovely as Mrs. Woodward would be sure to feel was appropriate, Kit gave in.

As she stood being pinned, tucked, and turned while Mrs. Danby, under Ava's close supervision, marked the hem of the cream-colored satin, Kit recalled the debacle of her graduation dress. The design of *this* dress was faultless, perfect for her tall, willowy figure. Remembering that other occasion naturally brought Cora Hansen to mind.

She and Dan rode out to the farm soon after Kit's return to see Cora, show her ring and tell their wedding plans. It saddened Kit to see Cora had slipped further and although she seemed to recognize Kit, her eyes were vacant and her manner lethargic.

On the way back to town, Kit wept a little and Dan tried to comfort her.

"She's in no pain, Kit, and her daughter-in-law is taking good care of her. Mrs. Hansen's had a hard life. Probably this is the most restful period of her entire life. I think she's contented and, whether or not she showed it, I am sure it pleased her very much to see you."

"I don't know." Kit sighed as she wiped her eyes. "I wish, somehow, I could have done more to make her happy."

"You can't be responsible for another person's happiness, Kit. You did more than you know to make Cora Hansen's life brighter, better, happier." He reached for her hand, drew it through his arm to hold it along with the buggy reins. "You do that for everyone whose life you touch, Kit."

Two days before the wedding Laurel arrived.

The two young women hugged, laughing and crying and exclaiming all at once when they saw each other.

"You look wonderful! Prettier than ever!" declared Kit, holding her friend at arm's length.

"And *you*, Kit! You were always beautiful! But *now* —" She shook her head. "Love! If they could only bottle it and sell it, it would make someone a fortune!"

They both giggled and hugged again and

ran upstairs to Laurel's bedroom, where Kit was happily ensconced. Settling down together on the windowseat like old times, they exchanged news, reminiscing and chatting as easily and naturally if they had never been apart. There was so much to share.

Ava almost hated to break in on the marathon conversation to tell them supper was ready. Afterward, Dan came by to welcome Laurel, then left again to let the two friends continue their reunion, uninterrupted.

Later, while getting ready for bed, Kit paused in front of the dressing table mirror. Putting down her hairbrush, she turned and looked her friend in the eye.

"The truth, Laurel?"

Laurel seemed surprised. "The truth? Well, of course. What is the question, Kit?"

"I — I know you loved Dan at one time —"

"Yes, I did." Laurel spoke decisively. "And I still do!"

Kit gave an involuntary gasp.

"But not the way you must be thinking," she hastened to say. "I love Dan as a sister loves a brother."

Still holding her breath, Kit pressed. "But tonight — when you saw him — were there any — well, any regrets?"

"Regrets? About *Dan?* Heavens no, Kit!" Laurel exclaimed. "I'm so happy for you both. Really and truly," she said earnestly, then went on. "If you knew Gene, you wouldn't have had to ask. Gene is exactly right for me just as Dan and you are exactly right for each other."

"It's just that when we were all in high school —" Kit blushed.

"Dear Kit, that was years ago! It seems a hundred now. Besides, if I had stayed here, not gone to Boston, I'd never have met Gene! That seems impossible now, but it's true. I wouldn't have found my grandmother either. And of course, it was through Gene that I was able to put together all the pieces of my life, find out about my real father."

Laurel came over and gave Kit a hug. "Ah, no, Kit, no regrets about anything. God had it all planned out for each of us. I believe that, don't you? And the way Dan looks at you, Kit, you should never have any doubts about *him*. I'm sure *he* has no regrets."

Kit returned her friend's hug gratefully. "I guess it's because I never really expected to have something this wonderful happen to me," she said slowly. "And lately so many good things have happened — I've had some success with my writing and now, Dan. It's almost too good to be true."

"I know, I used to feel that way at first

about Gene. I kept pinching myself to make sure I wasn't asleep and that I'd wake up and find I'd dreamed it all." Her eyes sparkled, then her lovely face grew serious. "It may have something to do with our being orphans, Kit. In the orphanage you're made to feel you're not important, you're just a number, a place in line, a cot in the dormitory — and then that awful thing of being paraded out in front of people, to be inspected like cattle!" She halted and for a moment they both relived that dreadful experience of the Orphan Train. Then with a little shudder Laurel went on.

"I *know* I was lucky being 'placed out' with the Woodwards, Kit. But you know it wasn't all easy. Mother was mourning their own daughter, Dorie, and I always felt I had to be better, brighter, nicer in order to be accepted. Even as a little girl I felt that pressure. And you know something else, Kit?" Here Laurel hesitated.

"What?"

"I was always afraid they'd send me back, that I'd do something terrible and have to go back to the orphanage!"

Kit shook her head slowly. "No, I didn't exactly worry about that, although I'm sure Jess might have been glad to get rid of me. In fact, I *hoped* sometimes that I *would* get sent back and maybe be 'placed out' somewhere else — especially when I saw the kind of homes you and Toddy had. Or, maybe, that my father would come looking for all of us — my little sister and brother — and we'd be a family again." Kit sighed. "I can't remember exactly when I gave up that dream!"

Laurel nodded sympathetically.

Kit wiped away the few tears that came and said brightly, "Oh, I haven't told you what happened after my article 'Little Lost Family' was published in *Woman's Hearth and Home* magazine, have I?"

She got out the letter from the woman who had adopted Gwynny, and let Laurel read it. They were just in the midst of an animated discussion when the bedroom door burst open unceremoniously and a voice sang out, "Surprise!"

Startled, they both turned and saw her standing in the doorway.

"Toddy!" they screamed in unison.

23

With the arrival of Toddy, the trio was complete. It was long after midnight when the three of them finally gave in to fatigue after the long day filled with excitement. Toddy departed for the Hale house, promising to be back early in the morning, and Laurel and Kit fell into bed and were instantly asleep.

The following afternoon, while Laurel practiced the solos she had been asked to sing at the ceremony, Toddy and Kit walked over to decorate the church for the wedding the next day. Both the Woodward and Hale gardens had supplied an abundance of brilliant fall flowers for them to use.

As they went up and down the aisles, tying wide satin white and gold ribbons in bows on the ends of each pew, Toddy and Kit had a chance to talk.

"I was so sorry to hear about Helene," Kit said softly.

"I know," Toddy replied. It was still hard for her to think about her adopted sister's death. "Of course, we all knew that it could happen any time. Her health was so delicate.

But I don't think I believed it until it actually happened!"

"It's easy to deny something you don't want to accept," agreed Kit, thinking of her own denial that her father had willingly abandoned them, chosen not to return, let them all be adopted. "But, in the end, life forces us to face even the unpleasant things."

"Yes." Toddy nodded, swallowing the hard lump that rose in her throat when she spoke of Helene. "Her death did make me come to some important decisions about my future. If she had lived, I don't think I would ever have gone into nursing. Mrs. Hale made everything so easy for us —"

"Is your training very difficult?" Kit asked, remembering the endless hard work of caring for Cora Hansen when she was ill.

"Yes, *very*. If I didn't feel it was what I was supposed to do, that it *was* my vocation, I don't think I could have gotten through the last two years. Now, I love it. It's given me a sense of purpose. The fact that I'm actually helping people who need me makes me feel worthwhile."

"And what about Chris, Toddy?" Kit asked gently.

Toddy took a long time arranging the bow she was tying before answering. "I sent him away, Kit. I didn't think it was fair to keep him dangling. Chris wanted me to run away with him and get married, in spite of his parents' objections. But knowing Helene might have only a short time to live — well, I'd already determined to devote the rest of my life to her."

"And you haven't been in touch with Chris since Helene died?"

Toddy shook her head. "I didn't give him any hope, Kit. I couldn't. I told him to find someone else —" She took out another length of ribbon. "Three years is a long time to wait for someone —"

"But you don't know that for sure, Toddy. Have you seen his mother?"

"Oh, Mrs. Blanchard!" Toddy shrugged, remembering the scene in the visitors' parlor at the Nursing School and from under the layers of self-protection, the buried humiliation and hurt surfaced. "No, and I certainly don't expect to. She would go to great lengths to avoid seeing me, Kit. She believes Chris is better off without me. And she may be right."

With that, Toddy picked up the box of ribbons and moved to the next pew.

In the tone of her friend's voice, Kit heard the edge of pain, and felt Toddy wanted the subject closed. But her sympathetic heart prayed that some day her friend would know the same kind of happiness she was experiencing. If not with Chris Blanchard, then with someone else who could love Toddy and whose love Toddy could return.

They finished decorating the rest of the church, then speaking of happier things, the two friends walked back to the Woodwards together.

Coming up the walk, Kit and Toddy heard Laurel's clear soprano voice ringing out. "Joy unspeakable and full of glory!"

Entering the house, they found Laurel at the piano in the parlor.

She looked up as they came in and greeted them gaily. "What other song do you want sung before the processional, Kit? 'O Perfect Love,' or —"

"What about 'The Lord's Prayer'?" Kit suggested. "I've heard you sing it and you do it so beautifully."

That evening the three gathered again up in Laurel's room. They were all rather quiet, knowing that this would be the last time they would be together in this particular way. Laurel would be returning to Boston, and Toddy had to leave right after the reception to go back to nursing school.

Suddenly Toddy broke the silence. "Do you remember what we promised each other when we were on the Orphan Train?"

"Of course!" Laurel exclaimed.

"That we'd be friends forever," Kit supplied.

"No matter what!" Toddy added.

"And we will," Laurel said firmly.

"Yes, but we're all going our separate ways now. Our lives are changing and expanding. Somehow we've got to find a way to stay in touch, not lose each other."

"Well, there are always letters."

"Yes, but it's so easy to put off writing, or even answering a letter. Time goes by, then it seems too much of an effort to try to catch up on everything that happens and gradually you let it slip by —" continued Toddy.

"What do you suggest then?" asked Kit, who found writing letters no task at all.

"I was thinking of a kind of round-robin letter," Toddy said. "We'd each write regularly, just jot down things we want to share, keep a sort of diary or journal. For example, I'd start it, say, when I get back to St. Louis, then mail it to Laurel in Boston. She'd add what she's been doing, then mail it to Kit here in Meadowridge. Kit would add her part and mail it back to me!"

"Wouldn't it get too long and bulky?" Laurel seemed puzzled.

"No, because when I receive Kit's version,

I'll delete my first entry, add a new one, and mail it on to you in Boston. I think it would work."

Each of them realizing how important it was to hold on to their oldest and dearest friendships, they agreed to give it a try.

Meadowridge Community Church was filled to capacity the following afternoon. An air of hushed expectancy stirred among the people who had crowded in to witness the marriage of their "young Doc" and his bride, one of their own.

As Kit, looking pale but radiant, came inside on Dr. Woodward's arm, they heard Laurel's sweet soprano raised in the words of the beautiful prayer set to music: "Our Father, which art in heaven, hallowed be Thy name —"

"Are you all right?" Dr. Woodward asked Kit anxiously, patting her hand.

"Yes, I'm fine," she reassured him.

Earlier, however, she had awakened, trembling with apprehension. For a few moments she lay in bed, staring at the early morning sunlight streaming into the room. It promised to be a lovely autumn day. Her wedding day!

Just then she heard a skittering sound and sat bolt upright as a few pebbles hit the windowpane and scattered onto the floor. She threw back the covers, jumped out of bed, and ran over to the window. There below, standing in the garden, was Dan.

Kit leaned on the windowsill and demanded in a stage whisper, "Dan! What are you doing here?"

"I couldn't sleep." He grinned up at her.

"But we're not supposed to see each other before the wedding. It's an old tradition."

"I had to come. See if you were really here. Do you love me? Are you going to marry me today?"

Kit suppressed the laughter bubbling up inside her and pressed both hands against her mouth. "Yes! I love you. And I am going to marry you today! Just *be* there," she called back to him.

"Just wanted to be sure." Dan chuckled, then blew her a kiss, and hands in his pocket, went whistling out through the gate.

That was the surprising, boyishly endearing side of Dan that few people saw in the usually serious young doctor. It was the part of him Kit loved most, knowing that she alone was allowed to see it. Dan had his own old childhood insecurities. But Kit knew they were both getting over the things that might have crippled them emotionally. Together they were learning to love and trust and depend on each other.

After that early morning secret encounter with Dan, all Kit's nervousness vanished. Ava, helping her dress, remarked that she had never seen a bride so serene and composed.

At the first chords of the classic wedding march, dozens of friendly, smiling faces turned to watch as Kit and Dr. Woodward started up the aisle.

Dan, looking tall and splendid in a dark suit, a boutonniere in his lapel, held out his hand to receive Kit as Dr. Woodward left her at the altar.

"O promise me that someday you and I —" Laurel sang as Kit placed her hand in Dan's and they moved together to join the Reverend Dinsmore.

Dr. Woodward stepped back and took his seat beside Ava, sitting in the first pew on the left, the place usually occupied by the bride's family. Well, that's what they were, *practically,* Dr. Woodward thought to himself, recalling vividly that moment of hesitation twenty-some years ago when he had stood with Laurel and seen Jess Hansen sign the adoption paper for Kit. He would never forget the forlorn look on the child's face, those big gray eyes wide with terror, as she had stood there holding her small cardboard suitcase. For one moment Lee's and Kit's eyes had met, hers in a mute plea for help. He remembered the strong urge he had felt to walk up to Jess and tell him he couldn't have Kit, that *he* was taking both little girls home with *him*. And then the thought of Ava and her reaction had he returned with, instead of the *boy* she had agreed to adopt, two little girls.

He had often regretted his lack of courage. Laurel had brought them so much happiness. Having Kit might have doubled it. Well, no use looking back. Kit had turned out well in spite of her joyless existence at the Hansens. And somehow he and Ava had been able to give her some of the love she may have lacked in that cold family.

And Dan, well if he couldn't have him as Laurel's husband, his *real* son-in-law, he was getting him as Kit's and as his associate in his practice, as well. Yes, God had blessed him mightily and he was grateful. Lee Woodward folded his arms and sat back to enjoy the ceremony.

Olivia Hale, seated right behind the Woodwards, looked admiringly at the petite figure of the maid-of-honor, charmingly dressed in apricot taffeta trimmed with velvet, perfect with Toddy's bright hair and coloring. Then her approving glance moved

258

over to Kit. She was certainly a stunning bride. The Brussels lace Olivia had brought back from France and given Kit for her veil was exquisite over her gleaming dark hair. Her eyes returned to Toddy. What a blessing the girl was, she sighed. Maybe she had taken her in out of pity and for the purpose of giving her invalid granddaughter a companion, but Toddy had proved so much more than that. Olivia recalled the trepidation with which she had brought Zephronia Victorine Todd from the station the day the Orphan Train had come. But she had been paid back a hundredfold. Her heart gave a small twinge as she thought that Toddy would have to leave on the evening train. Toddy was always a proverbial "ray of sunshine." Even after these few days, Olivia knew she would miss her. After only one more year of nurses' training, however, she would be back for good, Olivia hoped. She planned to make a large endowment to Meadowridge Hospital, where they needed to update the facilities and purchase new equipment. Perhaps that would prove an incentive to Toddy to practice her profession in a small town.

Gazing at Toddy's profile turned toward Kit and Dan as they took their vows, Olivia thought there was something wistful in her expression. Was it possible she still had romantic feelings for young Chris Blanchard? *No*, Olivia told herself comfortably. *I'm sure that was over before we left for Europe.*

From her vantage point in the choir loft, Laurel took in the entire scenario — the rapt well-wishers sitting in the pews, the lovely sanctuary transformed into a late-summer garden, the couple standing at the altar.

Her heart swelled with happiness for Kit. And Dan. Laurel was so grateful that he had found someone worthy of him, someone strong and independent and loving to be his helpmate and life's companion.

She hoped she had reassured Kit about any lingering feelings between Dan and herself. Laurel had never returned Dan's youthful infatuation for her. She had accepted it, enjoyed it, and cared for him as the brother she would never have. But she always felt as if she were waiting for her "real life" to begin, even though it was a vague, dreamlike vision of a far-away future. Dan's devotion had sheltered her as completely as the Woodwards' protective love. Neither, however, had prepared her very well for being on her own. That had taken courage that Laurel had called forth from some deep, hidden source within herself.

Remembering her Grandmother Maynard's

description of her real mother, Lillian, as "sweet-natured but strong-willed," Laurel had to smile. That could just as well describe *her!* It had hurt Papa Lee and Mother to discover that, but they had finally accepted it. She looked over at them affectionately and saw they were holding hands as they listened to the minister's words.

"Wilt thou have this man to be thy wedded husband, to live together according to God's ordinance in tile holy estate of matrimony?"

Unconsciously Laurel's lips formed the words, recalling adoringly how Gene had gazed at her, repeating that very same vow nearly two years ago. How lucky she was to have found him! Laurel thought, rejoicing. It was like finding the other part of herself. Together they were one, inseparable. "To love, honor and cherish, in sickness and in health, for richer or poorer, and forsaking all others, as long as you both shall live."

Suddenly Laurel couldn't wait to go "home" to Boston, to Gene. He had not been able to leave his teaching post at the Music Conservatory to accompany her on this trip to Meadowridge. It was lovely to be with Papa Lee and Mother, and to see Toddy, and be part of Kit's wedding, but Laurel knew her real place was with Gene.

"To have and to hold from this day forward —" Toddy looked down into the flowers of Kit's bridal bouquet she was holding during the ceremony, so that Kit's hands would be free when the couple exchanged rings.

It was Ava who had selected the combination of flowers for Kit to carry — white and yellow chrysanthemums, blue forget-me-nots, surrounded by myrtle leaves, arranged in a ruffle of tulle and tied with white satin streamers. Each flower had its own meaning — Ava had chosen them to represent Kit's special qualities of truthfulness, loyalty, constancy, and love.

"Having given each other a ring, the symbol of eternal love, and pledged to one another mutual respect, faithfulness and devotion before God and this congregation, I now pronounce you husband and wife."

A smiling Kit and Dan turned around, and Toddy handed Kit back her bouquet. At the sight of Kit's shining eyes, her look of absolute bliss, Toddy's heart turned over. Would *she* ever know such happiness?

Even though Kit was adept at putting emotions into words as a writer, she would have found it hard to express the deep feelings of that moment. After Dan slipped the wide, gold band on her finger and she heard

Reverend Dinsmore's solemn pronouncement, Kit felt exalted. Her feet simply did not seem to touch the floor as they started back down the aisle of the church.

Before her, she saw a sea of smiling faces. Many pairs of eyes, some of them brimming with tears, regarded her with warmth. She felt the flow of good wishes for her happiness sweeping toward her, enveloping her. Her throat ached with emotion.

Kit thought down all the long, lonely years that had led her to this moment and was overwhelmed with wonder and thankfulness. From somewhere in the back of her mind came the scriptural promise that was being fulfilled in her life today: "I will restore the years the locusts have eaten."

She felt the pressure of Dan's touch on her arm as they halted at the door of the church. "They want to take a picture of us here, darling."

Dazedly Kit looked down the steps where a man stood beside a cloth-draped camera on a tripod.

"That's wonderful! Stand right there, if you will. I want to get it just like that if you'll hold still for just one minute and keep smiling!"

Keep smiling? Kit felt as if she could never stop! There was an exploding sound as the photographer pressed his bulb.

"One more to be sure." They held still another minute. Then the man said, "Perfect! Thank you, Dr. and Mrs. Brooks."

The first time they had been addressed as "Dr. and Mrs. Brooks" registered in Kit's mind just as indelibly as the camera recorded the image of their first few moments as husband and wife on the steps of Meadowridge Church.

24

Kit looked up from her desk at the *Meadowridge Monitor* and took a deep breath. The wind blowing in from the open window was refreshingly fragrant with the smell of new spring blooms that had just begun to cautiously unfold in the park across the street from the old brick newspaper building.

She smiled to herself. After San Francisco, Meadowridge was a small town indeed, and coming back had not been all that easy for Kit. There were things about a rural setting she had not missed, but neither had she found in the city the things she *had* missed. Of course, in the end, it was because of Dan she had come back. She knew she loved him and wanted to spend the rest of her life with him. Now, a half year later, she had not regretted for a minute her decision to return.

Leaning her chin upon her hand, Kit tapped her teeth with the tip of her pencil and indulged in a little reminiscing.

They had not taken a wedding trip, but had gone after the reception at the Hale's to the repainted, refurbished house Dan's grandmother had left him. Ava had overseen the work, and every sparkling window, shining floor, polished surface welcomed Kit.

It still did not quite seem possible that all her dreams and hopes had come true, Kit sighed. The man she loved, a charming house, rewarding work. Life was altogether satisfactory and fulfilling.

Kit spent three afternoons a week at the *Monitor* and worked on her other writing at home. Since Dan was taking over more and more of Dr. Woodward's patients, especially those in the outlying areas and farms around Meadowridge, his hours were long and unpredictable. Kit could spend considerable time working on her writing without neglecting her new husband, his comfort or needs.

Her thoughts were interrupted by the arrival of the day's mail. Mr. Pennfold placed a stack of letters on her desk, tipping his cap and greeting her cheerfully.

" 'Morning, Mizz Brooks. Lorna over at the Post Office says you get more mail than anyone in Meadowridge. Reckon it's all that writing you do." He chuckled as he went out the door.

Kit shuffled through the envelopes. Most

of them were notices sent by the various clubs and social groups, or from church secretaries wanting publicity for their bazaar or bake sale or special meeting. There were several forwarded to her from the magazine. She was still hearing from readers about the "Orphan Train" story as well as some of her newer pieces published by *Woman's Hearth and Home.* It was gratifying to know that what she wrote was reaching so many people.

She often thought of the woman who had adopted Gwynny and written to her. She had shared the letter with Dan, and the photograph of her grown-up sister was mounted in a lovely silver frame and put in a place of honor on the mantle in their parlor.

Of course Jamie was still a question mark, and Kit often thought about her brother and prayed he was well and happy.

One afternoon, Kit was working alone in the office at the *Monitor.* It was Thursday, and since the paper had come out that morning, everyone else had gone home to a well-deserved rest. Kit, bent over the article she was writing, did not look up when she heard the front door open. It was probably Mr. Clooney, who found it hard to stay away from the newspaper more than a few hours, or perhaps Jessica, coming to check on something she'd forgotten.

It wasn't until a large shadow fell across her desk, blocking the sunlight, that Kit lifted her head.

Standing at a little distance from her was a man of medium height and muscular build, staring at her curiously. He wore a rough blue cotton shirt open at the neck, a many-pocketed sleeveless vest, faded indigo pants tucked into well-worn, dusty boots. Whipping off a battered, billed tweed cap, he shook back tousled sandy-colored hair and, ducking his head shyly, asked, " 'Scuse me, miss, but are you Miss Ternan?"

Kit frowned. She didn't recognize the fellow although there was something familiar about him.

"Yes."

He reached in his pocket, pulled out a folded paper, slowly opened its many-creased length and smoothing it out, held it up to her.

"You wrote this?"

Kit saw the head, "Little Lost Family," and nodded.

"Well . . . Kit, it's me. Jamie." A grin tugged at the corners of the rather cynical mouth in the weather-beaten face, wrinkled the corners of the eyes that were too old for twenty-five.

"Jamie?" she repeated.

"The same." The grin widened.

The pencil in Kit's fingers snapped and broke as her grip spasmed and she staggered, stumbling to her feet, holding onto the edges of the desk for support.

Suddenly came a rush of emotion, so powerful it stunned her. A torrent of feeling so intense she did not think she could contain it shuddered through her body, leaving her weak and shaking. After all her longing, all her pathetic wondering about her brother, here he was standing in front of her.

"Jamie! Jamie, how did you find me? Oh, Jamie!" she cried hoarsely.

"I was in St. Louis," he began. "And I seen this in the newspaper, reprinted it said from some magazine called *Woman's Hearth and Home*. I couldn't hardly believe it when I read it and realized it was about *us* and that you had written it!"

"Oh, Jamie, this is so wonderful! To think you found *me* when I've been praying for so long to find *you!*" Tears streamed down Kit's face and she held out both hands to him, wondering if he would mind if she hugged him.

His hands were workman's hands — calloused, the knuckles swollen and scarred, nails broken. Feeling their roughness, Kit wondered what kind of work Jamie did. But, first, there were other more important things.

"Come on, Jamie. We have so much to talk about, so much to catch up on — You must come home with me. I want you to meet my husband —"

"You married? But this byline says 'Ternan.' "

"That's my professional name, Jamie, the name I write under. But, yes, I'm married to someone I've known practically all my life. He's a doctor and we live just a few blocks over." Kit put on her sweater, picked up her hat, then tucked her arm through Jamie's. "Oh, I have so much to ask you, so many questions."

Soon they were seated in Kit's sunny kitchen. She put on the kettle to make coffee and sliced a large piece of apple pie for Jamie as she listened to his story.

"I was adopted out of Greystone by a nice, older couple who didn't have any kids of their own. They had a little farm upstate and I stayed with them about three years. I went to a country school and I even had a little pony to ride, chickens to feed. My chore was to gather the eggs every day. I liked it just fine." Jamie leaned his elbows on the table, one hand holding a forkful of apple pie, ready to pop into his mouth. "And . . . I guess you could say that was the end of the good times."

"What do you mean, Jamie?"

"Well, Mr. Heffner died and the old lady got real peaked and nervous-like, said she couldn't keep things goin' by herself. So a neighborin' farmer, a fellow named Gordon, bought her out lock, stock and barrel and took me along in the bargain. He didn't care nothin' about kids, just wanted extra hands, ones he didn't have to pay." Jamie scowled. "Worst thing that could have happened. If I'da known what it was gonna be like, I woulda run away right then."

"But what about Mrs. Heffner? Why didn't you go with her wherever she was going?"

"She felt bad about it, cried somethin' awful. She was gonna live with her sister and they already had four kids of their own, didn't want no more."

"So, then what happened?"

Jamie took another mouthful of pie before answering.

"I run away."

"When you were only . . . what . . . nine or ten? Oh, Jamie —"

"I don't know just how old I was at the time, but it wasn't too long after I stayed as long as I could take it at the Gordons. Talk about mean, Kit." Jamie shook his head. "And it weren't just me. He had another kid there workin' for him. He was about fifteen, and he'd been plannin' to escape — yeah, that's what he called it — like from a prison! He'd been stowin' stuff away for months, gettin' ready to do it. And I begged him to take me with him."

"This Gordon — what did he do?"

"You don't want to know, Kit." Jamie shook his head. "If I took my shirt off, you could see some of the scars 'cross my back where he used a buggy whip on me! I kicked and fought him but —" Jamie shrugged. "Well, what could a scrawny kid do against a growed man? He'd beat Tom a lot, too. That's why Tom was leavin.' "

"And so . . . did you?"

"Yep, we planned it real careful, tried it out a coupla times. We knowed when the freight train passed down at the edge of his farm, just when it slowed for the crossin' —"

"You rode the freight cars, Jamie?" gasped Kit.

"Plenty of times." He grinned, and curling his little finger daintily as he picked up the cup of coffee Kit had just refilled, Jamie put on an affected air. "In fact, I'd say it was my most frequent mode of transportation!"

"Oh, Jamie, what a life you've had. For a little boy to be alone, on his own like that —" She sighed, looking at him.

"Aw, it wasn't all bad, Kit. Sure it was tough, but there were other guys ridin' the rails. Some of 'em helped us out, taught us some of the tricks to survive, and me and Tom stuck together."

"So, you didn't get to go to school at all then, Jamie?"

"Not after I left the Heffners. But I've got along. One summer Tom and me got jobs with a carney — a travelin' carnival, doin' all sorts of odd jobs. We went all over, stayin' just a couple of days in every town, then movin' on. Got to see lot of the country, Kit. I liked it a lot. So, that's what I do, Kit. I'm a carney roustabout. It's a good life."

Kit's hands were clasped tightly in front of her on the table. Her throat felt hot and tight. She remembered the little brother whom she had taught his letters, and how to print before he was even five. She thought of the bright, inquisitive mind, how quickly he caught on to things, how much he had wanted to learn to read for himself, but loved for Kit to read to him. Jamie was smart. If he'd had an education, no telling how far he could have gone, what he might have become.

When Dan appeared, he welcomed Jamie warmly, said this certainly called for a celebration, and left again to go to the pharmacy and bring back a quart of ice cream for dessert. Kit was already preparing vegetables to go with the pot roast she had started earlier. The three of them sat around the kitchen table talking. Dan and Kit listened to Jamie's recital of his vagabond years, the interesting world of the carnival people of whom they knew nothing.

Dan was finally forced to leave them, saying he had surgery early in the morning, but Kit suspected he was tactfully leaving brother and sister alone for some more intimate sharing.

"I hope you plan to stay with us for a while, Jamie," Dan said as he shook his hand heartily before leaving the room.

Kit poured more coffee for each of them, then she and Jamie moved into the little parlor. She tossed some large pillows on the floor and they settled down in front of the fireplace where a small fire glowed cheerfully. Kit showed him Gwynny's picture and the letter from their sister's adoptive mother.

He read it through and when he handed it back, his eyes were glistening.

"Well, it looks like things turned out just

fine for her. I'm glad." They were both silent for a long moment, staring into the fire. Then not looking at Kit, Jamie slowly began to speak. "I found Da, Kit."

"You *did!* How, Jamie? Where?"

"When Mrs. Heffner packed me up to go over to the Gordon farm, she put in my adoption papers and I kept them. On them, they had Da's name and his address, at least what it was when he signed the release papers for me and Gwynny to be adopted. So, I just took a chance he might still be livin' in that area, near Brockton."

"So did you see him?"

"Yeah, I saw him." Jamie sounded grim. "I mean, I went by his house and found out where he worked. I'd seed some kids outside and thought maybe they wouldn't be too pleased for another kid — especially one who'd been ridin' the rails and didn't look so great — showin' up like that. So I waited for the end of his shift at the shoe factory and —"

"You spoke to him?"

"Sure. I recognized him but he didn't know me. Not at first, anyhow. I was pretty big, even at fourteen. It took him by surprise, that was for sure. He got kind of pale, then sort of started explainin' why he'd left us at Greystone, agreed to us gettin' adopted."

"Did he ask about Gwynny, or me?" Kit asked tentatively.

"He was sort of embarrassed, Kit, so I let him off the hook. I had thought of askin' him if I could spend the night at his house. A good home-cooked meal and a warm bed would have come in handy just then. But he stumbled around and said he'd married and there were some little kids —"

They were both quiet. Kit reached over and squeezed Jamie's big, rough hand.

"I guess there's nothin' to do but forgive him, Jamie."

"Sure, why not?" Jamie shrugged. "Poor guy. I guess he was up against it — out of work, three mouths to feed — Who's to say what anyone would have done?"

The clock on the mantle struck two before the brother and sister at last said good night. Kit had made up the bed in the downstairs bedroom that used to be Dan's when he was a boy and had lived here with his grandmother and aunts.

Kit hugged him before she went upstairs.

"I hope you will stay for a while, Jamie. I've just found you. I don't want to lose you again."

Jamie smiled but didn't say anything but, "Thanks, Kit, good night."

When Kit awakened the next morning,

the room was full of sunshine. She knew she must have overslept because the house was very still and quiet. She lay there for a minute, realizing Dan must have slipped out early to go to the hospital without waking her. And Jamie! In a rush of remembering all that had taken place the day before, Kit jumped out of bed, threw on her wrapper, and went down the stairway, tying her sash as she did.

"Jamie!" she called, looking for him first in the kitchen. Then she ran down the hall. The downstairs bedroom door was open, the bed stripped, the sheets and blankets neatly folded at the bottom. "Jamie!" Kit called again and her voice echoed through the empty house.

Slowly she walked back through the house and went into the parlor where they had sat and talked together for hours. On the mantle, propped up against the clock, was a folded paper. With a growing feeling of certainty, Kit went over and picked it up.

Dear Kit,

It was sure great to see you. I didn't want to say anything last night, but I had to leave at dawn to catch the train to where the carney is going to be next week. Don't be sad. Now that I know where you are, I'll be turning up again like that bad penny they talk about. You can count on it. You're some cook, Kit! Before too long I'll be seeing you.

Your brother, Jamie

PS. You got a fine husband. Tell him so long for me and thanks for everything.

Kit slipped the note into her pocket and went into the kitchen. Automatically she filled the kettle with water and put it on the stove to boil. She moved stiffly like someone in physical pain. Then suddenly great racking sobs welled up from deep inside her and she put her face in her hands and wept.

She wept for Jamie, for herself, for Gwynny, for all the lost years they might have had together, all that they might have given each other — the caring, the love, that irreplaceable threefold cord that bound them forever as a family.

The kettle's hissing alerted her that it had boiled dry. How many minutes had passed, Kit wasn't sure. She only knew that after the storm of weeping was over, a kind of calm settled over her. She lifted the kettle from the sizzling burner and refilled it.

Looking out the kitchen window into the backyard, she saw that the old apple tree had, seemingly overnight, put forth tiny pale green leaves. A full-breasted robin balanced on one bough. Spring's first promise.

As she stood there in the stillness, Kit realized her tears had done their healing work. Yes, it was only natural to grieve for what had been lost. But she knew in the fullness of her spirit, that every experience is for a purpose, and no matter how wrong or sad or tragic the original circumstances, God could use it for her good. Jamie had his path, Gwynny hers, Kit hers.

Suddenly it was as if Kit were seeing everything with new eyes. She realized she possessed all the essentials of happiness within the small sphere of this house, the beckoning garden, the bright April day. It would be ungrateful to a gracious Creator not to enjoy every minute allotted to her.

Kit took a deep breath, whispered a thankful prayer. The day stretched before her with countless opportunities for service, love and happiness.

She spent the morning planting vegetables for summer harvest. In the afternoon she took a favorite book of poetry outside and read, something she had not done in a very long time. Later she picked jonquils and grape hyacinths from Dan's grandmother's old-fashioned garden and arranged them in a Blue Willow pitcher and placed them on the dinner table. Then she fixed a casserole and salad, ready to serve whenever Dan arrived.

She had just done up her hair, put on a fresh blouse when she heard Dan's footstep on the porch and the front door open. As he stepped inside, he called, "Kit, Kit, I'm home!"

With a heart newly sure, she called back, "So am I! So am I!" and ran to meet him.